THE GODMOTHER

THE GODMOTHER

▼

First Lady of the West

Charles O. Goulet

Writers Club Press
San Jose New York Lincoln Shanghai

The Godmother
First Lady of the West

Writers Club Press
an imprint of iUniverse.com, Inc.

For information address:
iUniverse.com, Inc.
5220 S 16th, Ste. 200
Lincoln, NE 68512
www.iuniverse.com

ISBN: 0-595-19281-5

Printed in the United States of America

I dedicate this book to my wife, Denise, who has supported my writing by giving me the time to pursue it and to her proofreading skills and patience as she corrects my many errors in grammar, spelling, and punctuation.

CONTENTS

FOREWORD

This is the remarkable story of Marie Anne Lagimodiere who was the first white woman to make her home in the great Northwest of Canada. She was the first of many that would follow her to make their homes in the wilderness and to help populate Western Canada, one of the greatest places on earth to live.

CHAPTER ONE

THE GREAT ROMANCE

▼

Marie-Anne stared out the paned window. The dark scudding clouds matched her mood. It was Friday, August 2, 1805—her twenty-fifth birthday—and she was depressed and unhappy.

"Marie-Anne, it's time to work…not to dream of a knight in shining armour who'll arrive in the rain and whisk you off to some exciting foreign country. Here, take these sheets and go make Monsieur le Cure's bed."

Although she spoke sharply, Marie-Anne knew that Madame Frenier, the middle-aged housekeeper, was kind by nature, and she treated Marie-Anne like the daughter that she'd never had. Marie-Anne shrugged her shoulders in resignation and stood for several more moments looking out onto the single dirt track that was the main street of the tiny village of Maskinonge, Lower Canada. All her life, this was the only place that she knew. True, every couple years, she made the trip to Three Rivers, the bustling town twenty kilometres east at the mouth of the St. Maurice River where it emptied into the mighty St. Lawrence. That was an exciting time. The town was always busy with lumbermen from the northern forests, miners from the nearby iron mines, and fur-traders from the north and the west. Oh, how the men seemed to enjoy life—laughing, joking, and talking excitedly among themselves. Sometimes Marie-Anne wished that she had been born a boy rather than a girl. Then she could do all the exciting and wonderful things that boys were allowed to do but which girls were not.

Madame Frenier's sharp "Marie-Anne!" brought her out of her reverie.

"Sorry. I'm on my way."

"My, Marie-Anne, you're not yourself this morning. What's the matter? Are you sick?"

"No, Madame. I was just thinking that it's almost ten years that I've been working at the presbytery. That's a long time."

Madame Frenier laughed. "My dear, you're still young. You've many years ahead of you. I've been working for the priests of this parish for over twenty years."

"That is a long time. Don't you ever feel like leaving and going to another part of the world?"

"I did at one time, but it's too late now. I'm forty-five years old and this is all I know—to cook, to wash, to take care of the priests."

Marie-Anne thought she sounded a little wistful. "Did you ever think of getting married…and doing all those things for your own family—a husband and some children?"

"Yes, years ago I thought of that, but now it's too late. But it's not too late for you, Marie-Anne."

Marie-Anne cocked her head. "If I don't meet a young man soon, it will be too late for me too."

The older woman shook her head. "That may be true, Marie-Anne. There aren't too many young men left in Maskinonge. Most have gone to find work elsewhere. There's not much to do in Maskinonge these days. All the good land's been taken, there are no animals in the woods, why, even the best trees have been cut down. So the young men look for their fortunes elsewhere."

Marie-Anne shook her head sadly. "Those that I want aren't available, and those that want me the devil wouldn't want."

Madame Frenier smiled at the remark. "Maybe you've been too picky. There's still Gabriel Dupont. He's still available, and he's well established on his farm."

Marie-Anne wrinkled her nose in disgust. "He's old enough to be my grandfather. I'd never think of him."

Madame Frenier laughed heartily. Dupont wasn't old enough to be her grandfather, but he could have been her father. He was more Madame's age than Marie-Anne's.

At that moment the priest, Monsieur l'Abbe Vinet-Souligny, entered the small kitchen of the presbytery. Both woman started in surprise. Marie-Anne's face reddened as she wondered if the old priest had overheard their conversation.

"Good morning, ladies. Would it be possible to get a cup of tea. The weather's depressing, and maybe a cup of tea will cheer me." He rubbed his hands together as was his habit.

Marie-Anne picked up the sheets from the chair on which they lay and quickly left the room. As she hurried down the hall to the priest's bedroom at the far end, she could hear the murmur of voices as the two older persons talked. She hoped they weren't discussing her.

Twenty-five years old today, she mused. A quarter of a century and she wasn't married yet. All the girls her age had found a husband, and most were already mothers, some with several children. What was the matter with her? She was pretty enough. Her blonde hair and grey eyes emphasized her broad forehead and her rosy cheeks. She was of medium height and sturdily built—strong and healthy, like her brothers and sisters.

Her father, Charles Gaboury, worked his small farm a few miles outside the village, and although they had never been wealthy, they never lacked the necessities of life. At sixteen, she left her father's home, and since that time she had worked for the parish priest as a helper to his housekeeper, Madame Frenier. Somehow, working for the priest had scared the young men away, and she'd never had a boy friend, let alone a beau. Maybe that was the problem. Maybe she should seek work elsewhere. But jobs were scarce in Maskinonge, and her parents wouldn't approve of a move to Three Rivers or Quebec, and Montreal was out of the question. It was too big and too dangerous for a woman by herself. "What should I do?" she muttered to herself. "There are no young men for me here."

Two days later, on Sunday, Marie-Anne, along with the people of the village of Maskinonge and the surrounding farms, went to Mass in the parish church. Sunday was Marie-Anne's day off, and often she went home to spend the day and to enjoy her mother's homecooked dinner.

It was a bright day, full of sunshine and fine weather, and everyone was in a jovial mood. Although the service had been long and the Latin ceremony dull, Marie-Anne enjoyed the singing of the choir. She often wished she had a good singing voice, but unfortunately her singing talent was lacking.

After Mass, people stood around in small groups exchanging news and gossip and visiting with friends they hadn't seen all week. The farmers discussed the progress of their crops and the prices they expected from the sale of their livestock, particularly the hogs and sheep. Few of them had many heads of cattle—most of these were kept to increase the size of their herds.

Marie-Anne joined her family who wished her a belated happy birthday. Birthdays were seldom celebrated in a special way, particularly if they occurred in mid-week. No one had time to neglect the work that had to be done.

Her father teased her. "Marie-Anne, my little one, another year has passed and you're not married yet."

Marie-Anne wrinkled her nose. She was a bit annoyed. "Oh, Papa, I'm getting too old for that kind of teasing."

He laughed and leaned toward her, placing his lips next to her ear. "There's an old friend of yours back in the country. He's been asking about you."

"Who's that, Papa?"

"Someone who left five years ago. Now he's back from the 'pays d'en haut'. Do you remember Jean-Baptiste Lagimodiere? I think he's a couple years older than you."

"Of course I remember him. He was always teasing me and pulling my pigtails. What's he doing back here?"

"Well, to tell you the truth, I think he's looking for a wife." Her father chuckled and his eyes twinkled.

"He's come to the wrong place. I'm the only old maid left. Is he at Mass?"

Her father slowly surveyed the knots of churchgoers, and finally he spotted what he was looking for.

"See. He's over there, talking with the Bergeron boys."

Marie-Anne followed her father's glance. A medium height, stocky man with newly-trimmed light brown, almost blond hair, stood in lively conversation with several other young men. He was waving his arms and hands vigorously and seemed to be telling an intriguing story to his attentive audience. When he had finished, the group exploded into laughter. Several slapped him on the shoulders in appreciation. He hadn't changed much in five years—perhaps he had filled in and was more mature. The upper part of his face was sun-tanned and windburned as if he spent a great deal of time outdoors. He was clean-shaven, but the lower part of his face had a pallor that indicated that he'd recently removed a beard. He wore a black felt hat with a high crown, and he looked uncomfortable in the white shirt with its starched collar. Even the wide cravat at his neck seemed out of place. Marie-Anne could not see the rest of his clothes, but they seemed new and not yet fitted to his sturdy body.

At that moment, he swung around, and their eyes met. A shadow of a smile played around the corners of his mouth as he turned back to the men he was talking to. Marie-Anne could feel her cheeks become hot, and she was sure that she was blushing.

Her father whispered, "Well, what do you think of him? He seems to have prospered in the West. He tells me there are many opportunities there. The North West Company and the English company...what's the name?…oh, yes…the Hudson's Bay Company is always looking for good men. It seems they need canoeists, hunters, trappers, and traders. Jean-Baptiste has been working for the North West Company. The wages have been good, and now I think he's ready to settle down."

"Oh, Papa, are you that eager to get rid of me? You know I'll only marry someone I love."

"Would you like to meet Jean-Baptiste? I'll ask him over for dinner. Today, even."

Her brothers and sisters were all in favour of the idea and indicated their agreement noisily, much to Marie-Anne's discomfort, for she feared the young man would hear what was going on. She nodded in agreement; her father smiled.

Jean-Baptiste was an entertaining fellow: throughout the meal he amused them with tales of derring-do on the trail, with humourous incidents among the Indians of the West, and stories about the strange buffalo of the Plains. A smile was never far from his lips, and his eyes twinkled in merriment. He appeared to be a man who was happy with his lot in life. Many times that afternoon Marie-Anne felt his clear blue eyes on her; she felt flattered. He obviously was interested in her, and her family did not fail to notice it. The younger ones giggled and shyly looked from Marie-Anne to the exciting voyageur from the far West.

As the late afternoon shadows lengthened, Marie-Anne turned to her father. "Papa, I'll soon have to be going back to the presbytery. You know, it's a good hour drive."

Usually they had an early supper, and then her father would drive her back to the village in the early evening.

Jean-Baptiste spoke. "If you don't mind, Monsieur Gaboury, I'd like to drive Marie-Anne home."

"Jean-Baptiste, that's up to Marie-Anne, and I'm sure Pierre won't mind being your chaperone."

Pierre was Marie-Anne's older brother who had spent two years in the West as a voyageur for the North West Company. He had not found the work to his liking so he had returned to his father's farm.

Pierre turned to Marie-Anne. "I'll go hitch up the horse and buggy. It won't be long."

In the next months, Marie-Anne saw Jean-Baptiste often, for it soon became apparent to the whole community that he was attracted to her. Throughout the winter, he was a regular Sunday visitor in the Gaboury household. Since he came from a good local family, his attentions were not discouraged by the family. As for Marie-Anne, she wasn't sure of her feelings toward the gallant and audacious hunter from the West.

She had to admit that she enjoyed his attentions, and as she got to know him better, she realized that she found him attractive. He was a pleasant, happy, jovial man with a strong sense of humour and a ready smile. Everyone liked Jean-Baptiste Lagimodiere—the young men his age, the older men, the older women, and, as well, many of the younger girls. It was apparent to Marie-Anne that he had the choice of almost any woman he wanted. But he seemed to prefer Marie-Anne.

As the new year arrived, Marie-Anne knew that soon Jean-Baptiste would ask her to marry him. She would have to make a decision. She liked Jean-Baptiste—she liked him very much—but she wasn't sure she loved him. There were a number of things that bothered her about him.

The third Sunday in March was a warm day with the deep snows of winter beginning to melt. Marie-Anne had, as usual, spent the afternoon at the family farm. That evening Jean-Baptiste drove her, with the horse and cutter, back to the presbytery. Dusk came early at this time of year, and the moon and stars shone crisply from the brilliant sky. The air was sharp as the horse trotted smoothly along the narrow trail leading to the village.

Throughout the day she noticed that Jean-Baptiste was more subdued than usual. Her intuition warned her that something was on his mind. As they approached the village, it bothered her so much that she turned to him. "What's the matter, Jean-Baptiste? You've been very quiet today. Are you angry with me?"

He stammered hurriedly, "No, no, Marie-Anne, you've done nothing. It's I…I've been doing some thinking."

"My, it must be serious to make you so quiet."

"I must think of my future. Soon it'll be time to go back to the West. The brigades will be leaving as soon as the ice has left the rivers, and I must decide whether I'll join them or look for a place here in Maskinonge or someplace nearby. I've enough money saved to buy a small farm and become a settled 'habitant', but I'm not sure that's what I want to do. Marie-Anne, I've an important question to ask you. Your answer will help me to make my decision."

"Well, Jean-Baptiste, I hope I can help you. What's your question?"

Jean-Baptiste looked straight ahead to the back of the cantering horse. The jingling of the harness bells was pleasant music to his ears, and the crunch of the iron shod sleigh runners added its counterpoint to the bells. The silence between them became tense. Finally he turned to her and said in a low voice, "Marie-Anne, would you do me the pleasure of becoming my wife?"

A long pause followed. "Jean-Baptiste, I like you very much. In fact, I think I love you. But I must know your plans before I answer you. If you plan to run away to the West, I don't think I can marry you. I don't want a husband who's never at home. That's not a home."

"You see, Marie-Anne, that's my problem. If you'll marry me then I'll look for a place here; if you won't marry then I'll go back to the West. There are more opportunities there than here. You see, everything depends on your answer."

"I cannot answer you tonight."

The next week was a tense one for Marie-Anne. Jean-Baptiste had not been pleased with her answer, but she had decided that she wouldn't be married in name only. She wanted her husband to be with her. That was the way God had planned marriage to be—two people living together as one, like her parents.

Each day she hoped Jean-Baptiste would come to her and tell her that he was prepared to settle down in Maskinonge, but he never came. She realized that she loved him. He was never very far from her mind. She could see his smiling face and hear his musical voice, deep and resonant.

On Sunday she expected to see him at her parents' farm, but he didn't appear. He wasn't at Mass either. She wondered if he'd already left for the West. When she asked Pierre, he replied, "He told me he was going to Montreal to see about his old job with the North West Company, but he also said he was going to look at a farm not far from Montreal. What did you tell him? He told me that he asked you to marry him, but you wouldn't give him an answer. You know, Marie-Anne, he's a good man. I'm sure he'll always take good care of you. He loves you very much."

Marie-Anne looked at Pierre solemnly. "Yes, I'm sure of that, but I don't want a husband who's always away from home."

The following Monday afternoon Marie-Anne was called to the door of the rectory. To her surprise, there stood Jean-Baptiste. He was dressed in his Sunday best.

"May I speak to you, Marie-Anne?" he asked quietly.

"Of course, Jean-Baptiste. I'm very happy to see you. I missed you greatly yesterday."

"Oh, I had business in Montreal."

"So Pierre told me. Did you get it done?"

"Yes and no. I can have my old job back anytime I want it. But I was looking for a farm as well. I'm not sure I'll get it, but it looks promising. Marie-Anne, have you thought of my proposal. Will you marry me?"

"Jean-Baptiste, I thought of it a great deal. I've spent several sleepless nights because of it. But I've made my decision."

CHAPTER TWO

THE BIG DECISION

▼

Monday, April 21, 1806, was a warm, sunny day in the tiny village of Maskinonge. The entire parish turned out for the marriage of Marie-Anne Gaboury and Jean-Baptiste Lagimodiere. It was the right time of the year for a grand celebration. Most of the snow had disappeared under the rays of the spring sun, but the fields were not yet ready for the spring planting. The ice had not broken on the rivers; the land was in a state of anticipation, so everyone took the day off from their work to witness the great event in the lives of these two young persons.

The ceremony, part of the Nuptial Mass, was simple, and immediately afterwards, relatives and close friends went to the Gaboury farm where a sumptuous dinner and an afternoon of partying took place. Marie-Anne's face glowed as she received the well-wishes from her friends and relatives. She was no longer the old maid of the parish. Jean-Baptiste looked pleased with himself; he'd found the wife who would make him happy. She was a handsome, healthy women, strong-willed yet kind and understanding.

The first days of their married life were ideal, but as the days lengthened and April turned into May, Marie-Anne noticed a change in Jean-Baptiste. He was still the loving, attentive young bridegroom, but he was restless and preoccupied. She even noticed that at times he was irritable. She knew he was concerned about their future: the farm near Montreal that he'd tried to buy was sold to someone else. Although she was still working at the presbytery, she knew the job would soon be someone else's. After all, she now had a husband to support her.

One evening in early May, as they sat on the veranda of the small house which they rented, Jean-Baptiste turned to her and said, "Marie-Anne, if I don't find something soon, I think I'll return to the West. I'm getting tired of working for others for poor wages. I can't find a decent job, and the farms are far too expensive to buy."

Shock covered her face, and her right hand went to her throat. "We've been married only two weeks, and already you're talking of leaving me!"

He looked sadly at his new wife. "I'm sorry, my love, but I just don't see a future for us here. Tomorrow I think I'll go to Three Rivers and see if I can find a job there."

"That's a good idea, my husband." She spoke lovingly and smiled as she evaluated his remark. She knew that he was a good worker with many talents. She had seen him work on her father's farm; whenever there was something to do, he was quick to offer his services. As well, he was an excellent hunter and woodsman. She was sure he would find a suitable job. She reached across and squeezed his hand. He pressed hers in return.

A deep smile creased his dark face and he bent forward. "Marie-Anne, why don't you get the day off tomorrow and come with me to Three Rivers. We'll make it a little honeymoon, and at the same time I'll look for work."

Marie-Anne's face lit up, and she pulled his hand to her mouth and kissed it. "That's a wonderful idea. It's a long time since I've been to Three Rivers. I like to go there. It's full of excitement and adventure. I've even a few sous saved for just such an occasion."

Jean-Baptiste laughed joyfully. He was always amazed at the way his new wife considered anything out of the ordinary as an adventure. He also admired the way in which she was willing to try anything new. No doubt it was her adventurous spirit and her self-confidence that attracted him to her.

The next morning, early, Jean-Baptiste borrowed a horse and a cart from one of his friends in the village, and the newly-weds were on their way to the town of Three Rivers. The road along the north bank of the St. Lawrence River was in good condition for this early in the spring, and they enjoyed the three hour drive to the town. As they made their way, Jean-Baptiste joined Marie-Anne in her excitement.

Many puddles still filled the road, and the numerous streams that flowed into the St. Lawrence were high and swift-flowing. As they crossed one of the wooden bridges over these streams, Jean-Baptiste remarked, "If we were in the West there would be no bridge, and we'd be forced to swim across these streams. It's exciting. You take off your clothes, tie them into a bundle, and attach them to your horse. Then you make the horse enter the stream and hold onto him as he swims across."

Marie-Anne laughed heartily. "What if the horse gets away and leaves with your clothes?"

He laughed. "Oh, it happens. Then you hope it's not too cold, and that you can find something to cover your nakedness. Everyone will have a good laugh if you must borrow clothes from someone."

"Has that ever happened to you?"

"No, my sweet, I'm much more careful than that. But I've heard stories of similar happenings. Often one falls through the lake or river ice in the springtime. That's worse. The water's very cold, and if you can't make a fire or get to shelter, you can freeze to death very quickly."

"Did that ever happen to you?" Her voice filled with concern, and a worried look covered her face.

He grinned mischievously. "Oh, often. Then I would be rescued by the Indian girls."

Marie-Anne slapped him playfully, and he urged the horse to a quicker pace for they could see the outskirts of Three Rivers. The town of Three rivers was located on a point of land that jutted into the St. Lawrence River and was strung along the north shore westward for three-quarters of a mile. The St. Maurice or Three Rivers, which it was often called as there were two islands at its mouth which divided it into three channels, flowed here into the St. Lawrence. It was an old town having been founded in 1677 by the bishop of Quebec.

Marie-Anne pointed to the tall spire of the Catholic church that dominated the town. "You know, Jean-Baptiste, many times I thought I might join the convent of Ursuline nuns and devote my life to the poor and the sick."

"I'm glad you didn't."

They followed the rutted main street that paralleled the St. Lawrence River. As they approached the centre of the town, the residential homes gave way to the commercial establishments. Along each side of the main street were shops and stores. Jean-Baptiste pointed out the large warehouse of the North West Company, and then they passed the blacksmith shop with its glowing forge and the numerous wagons, carts, and sleighs—some of them waiting to be fixed, while others waited the return of their owners to pay for the repairs that had been done to them. Marie-Anne wrinkled her nose at the acrid smell of charred hoofs as the blacksmith worked at shoeing a horse.

Jean-Baptiste noticed her displeasure and teased, "That's a pleasant smell compared to the smell of the guts of many animals being butchered during a buffalo hunt."

"I don't think I'd like that!"

"It isn't pleasant, but it's necessary."

The horse slowed to a leisurely walk. Marie-Anne enjoyed the sights of the town. Jean-Baptiste pointed to his left, indicating the main channel of the St. Maurice River. "There's an iron foundry about nine miles out of town. I think I'll see if they're hiring any men. They've an office here in town. But first we must go to the inn for something to eat."

The sun was high in the sky, and they hadn't eaten since early morning. He located an inn along the main street, drew up in front of it, and tied the horse to the hitching rail, which was nothing more than a horizontal pole set atop two posts, one at each end. He lifted Marie-Anne from the gig and deposited her on the wooden sidewalk that fronted the weather-beaten frame building. After he tended the horse with a portion of hay and a dollop of oats that he carried in the back of the cart, he joined Marie-Anne.

They entered a low, dimly-lit room as the only illumination was two small windows that faced the street. A half dozen small, heavy, square tables were scattered in a regular pattern throughout the room.

They paused at the door to allow their eyes to adjust; then Jean-Baptiste steered her to one of the tables at the window. The other was occupied by a man who had his back to them. Marie-Anne noticed that his dark hair was long and curled over the collar of his coarse-woven, dull-coloured shirt. He was hunched over his plate, eating noisily as if he was not used to eating in such places.

Jean-Baptiste gallantly held the heavy chair for her, and she sat with her back to the man at the next table. Jean-Baptiste took the seat across from her.

At that moment a loud, coarse voice boomed across the room. "Do you want to drink or to eat?"

The suddenness of it startled Marie-Anne, and she searched the dim recesses of the room to find its source. A large, heavyset woman in a long skirt of coarse stuff materialized out of the dimness. Almost like an ogre, Marie-Anne mused.

The woman came across the room quickly, a wide smile twisting the corners of her mouth.

Jean-Baptiste grinned at the woman. "How's Jeanette today?" he asked familiarly.

"Well, well, if it isn't Jean-Baptiste Lagimodiere, back from the 'pays d'en haut'. How are the Indian maidens there?"

Before Jean-Baptiste could answer, the man at the next table turned quickly, and still chewing his food exclaimed, "Well, if it isn't my old friend, Jean-Baptiste, the Great Hunter. What are you doing here in Three Rivers?"

The two men rose, and the large woman moved back a step as they came together in a bear hug. They clasped each other joyfully and slapped each other vigorously on the back. They laughed and pumped each other's hand. Marie-Anne stared at the two men in astonishment. Who was this man who greeted her husband so familiarly? He wasn't anyone she knew. He didn't seem to be from Three Rivers either.

Jean-Baptiste swung his friend to face Marie-Anne. "This, Pierre, is my new wife, Marie-Anne. Marie-Anne, this is my good friend, Pierre Boucher, from the 'pays d'en haut', the West. He's a voyageur and hunter of the north, a place called Isle-a-la-Crosse. This man's the greatest voyageur of the Northwest."

Marie-Anne surveyed the man; he was short but powerfully built. His shoulders were massive seeming to burst from the short cloth coat that he wore. A single button closed it at the top, and his ample stomach protruded from the opening below. His coarse shirt was open just above the waist of his pants, and a small portion of his hairy stomach showed through. His dark pants were too short in the leg and revealed his feet and a good part of his ankles which were encased in deep tan moccasins with brightly beaded insteps. He reached for Marie-Anne's hand; she noticed his hands were large and strong. He took her hand gently in his, lifted it to his lips, and kissed it lightly.

"My pleasure, Madame. I'm happy for Jean-Baptiste. He's chosen a beauty."

Marie-Anne blushed and murmured, "Thank you." Then he turned back to Jean-Baptiste, ignoring her totally.

"I didn't know you were in this part of the world, my friend. What are you doing…besides getting married?"

"Well, Pierre, I'm here looking for work."

"You're in luck, my friend. I'm here looking for men. I've just the job for you, Jean." Pierre Boucher was the only person who called him simply "Jean"; to everyone else he was "Jean-Baptiste." "Will you join me at my table?"

Marie-Anne looked at Jean-Baptiste with imploring eyes. She preferred to eat alone with him, but he did not see her look, or if he did, he chose to ignore it. Unceremoniously, he helped her move to his friend's table.

During the ensuing meals, the two men ignored Marie-Anne as they reminisced about friends they knew and the activities of the two main companies in the West—the Hudson's Bay Company and the North West Company. One of these events was the move of the North West Company's headquarters from Grand Portage to Fort Kaminsitikwia at the western end of Lake Superior.

Later, Jean-Baptiste told Marie-Anne to explore the few shops on main street while he looked for work. She felt abandoned as she watched her husband and Pierre Boucher turn in the opposite direction, and, engrossed in conversation, make their way up the street. She was more hurt when they didn't turn back to wave to her, but she tried to cheer herself up as she murmured, "I guess I can't expect him to give up all his bad habits so soon. I'll have to be patient." Then she smiled as she anticipated an afternoon of roaming through the shops looking at the beautiful clothes from the big cities of Quebec and Montreal. It would be fun even if she didn't plan to buy too much.

Dusk had descended upon the town when she met Jean-Baptiste at the rig. His friend had disappeared yet Marie-Anne noticed that Jean-Baptiste was in a jovial mood. As they travelled westward on the road back to Maskinonge, he talked incessantly about his life on the western plains. He was excited and animated.

"Marie-Anne, have you ever seen a 'canot de maitre', the big freight canoe that's used to carry goods in the Indian trade? They're big, Marie-Anne…at least forty feet long and six feet wide, and they have a crew of ten or twelve, a 'gouvernail' or steersman, an 'avant' or bowman, and eight or ten paddlers or voyageur…and they carry between four and five tons of goods…and through the roughest water in the world."

"No, I've never seen a canoe like that…just the ordinary small canoe."

He continued, the excitement in his voice increasing, "It's thrilling to shoot the rapids in such a canoe…the crew must work together as one…one mistake and…swoosh, everything is lost—the cargo, and sometimes even lives."

Marie-Anne was shocked at the indifferent way in which he talked about the danger involved, but she remained silent.

"But the buffalo hunt is the best. You should see the herds. They are so large they stretch for miles. One rides into it and picks the animal he wants, chases it, shoots it, and goes on to the next. If the herd should panic and stampede, then it can be very dangerous."

"Have you ever been in such a stampede?"

"Oh, yes. And I tell you it's impressive. Marie-Anne, you can't imagine how stimulating it is."

Marie-Anne could tell by the feeling in his voice that he missed that kind of life. For several moments they rode along in silence; Jean-Baptiste turned to her. He stared at her, searching her face. Marie-Anne could feel the tension, and a shiver went up her back.

"What is it? Why are you staring at me so?"

The intensity in his face frightened her.

"Marie-Anne, I've something very important to tell you." He paused. "I've taken a job with the North West Company as a voyageur. I'll be leaving for the West the first week in June."

Her mouth dropped open; her eyes widened; she clenched her fists; her breath caught. For several moments she gazed at Jean-Baptiste in astonishment. Then she spoke. "Jean-Baptiste, I can't believe you've done this without talking to me about it. You'll be gone for a long time?"

"I'll be gone until Fall when the brigade returns to Montreal with a cargo of furs."

Tears came to her eyes, but she fought them back. She wouldn't let him see how hurt she was.

He put his arm around her shoulders and drew her close. "My sweet, it's for our future. The pay's good, and when I come back, I'll have enough money to do whatever we want."

"But, Jean-Baptiste, I'll be alone for more than half a year. That's not a marriage. Please stay with me."

"Marie-Anne, I can't. There's nothing to do here. There's no work. There's no money. There's nothing. I must go."

Marie-Anne noticed the determination in his voice. How could she change his mind? She was sure that no matter what she said, he wouldn't listen to her. His mind was made up. The rest of the trip home was made in silence, each immersed in thought.

The die was cast.

But during the following days, Marie-Anne did everything she could to get him to change his mind. She begged, she pleaded, she argued, she threatened, but the only thing that happened was that she discovered Jean-Baptiste was a determined man: when he made up his mind, nothing would change it.

As a last resort, she prayed. She attended Mass daily, and she recited the rosary often, sometimes several times a day, but not even that could change Jean-Baptiste's mind.

One day as she knelt in a pew at the back of the church praying, a thought struck her.

That evening as they sat at the table enjoying the supper Marie-Anne had prepared, she gazed at Jean-Baptiste and smiled sweetly. "Jean-Baptiste, I've come to a decision too."

His hand, with a forkful of food, stopped halfway to his mouth. He froze, his mouth half open. What had his wife decided? "Whatever you've decided sounds very important."

"I think it is," she replied solemnly.

Several thoughts flitted through his mind. Was his wife to have a baby? But that would hardly be a decision. It would be a fact, or it wouldn't be a fact. Was she about to leave him because he was going to the West for the summer? Or had she decided where she was going to live while he was away?

"I've decided to go West with you."

"What did you say?" He wasn't sure that he'd heard her properly.

"I'm going with you. A wife belongs with her husband."

He was silent. Then he said, "But...that's impossible. You can't come with the brigade."

"Why not?"

"Because...because it's never been done. It's too dangerous. It's too risky."

"I'm going, Jean-Baptiste. You can't change my mind. I've thought about it carefully. I could be of great help to you as we're travelling—I can cook the meals...I can make camp...I can look after your clothes, I can..."

"No, Marie-Anne, it's impossible. That trip's no place for a woman. It's difficult. The hours are long. The weather's often bad. The portages are dangerous. No!"

"Jean-Baptiste, I'm healthy and strong. I'm as tough as any man."

Jean-Baptiste smiled. She was hardly a match for any man. Some of those voyageurs were incredibly strong. He had seen some of them carry three and four pieces, which were the ninety pound packages into which the trade goods or fur were packed. Most men carried only two pieces at a time, and that was thought to be a good load.

"I'm going, Jean-Baptiste. Nothing will change my mind just as nothing will change your mind."

He could see she was determined. "It's never been done before...but...maybe you're right. Maybe we can be the first." He was humouring her: he didn't think that she'd insist on going after she'd slept on the idea.

But he was wrong.

The next Sunday she told her family of her plan to go with Jean-Baptiste. They were shocked and opposed the idea. They tried to dissuade her, but she wouldn't change her mind. Even Pierre, her brother who'd been to the West, begged her to reconsider, but to no avail. Her mother suggested that she talk to the parish priest about her plan. She agreed.

On Tuesday of the following week she told Monsieur l'Abbe what she planned to do, and she was surprised when he agreed with her even though he pointed out the dangers and hardships, and he also included the idea of a permanent residence there. If that happened, she must remember that there would be no priests, no churches, and no schools for her children.

She laughed. "Oh, Monsieur l'Abbe, it's only for the summer. We'll be back in the fall. We'll make our fortune and then come home to establish ourselves."

"You may be right, but sometimes God has other plans."

Marie-Anne found the carriage trip to Montreal interesting, but she found the city more exciting. The people seemed so busy as they rushed from building to building, and carriages, carts, and wagons of every shape and size moved purposefully through the main streets. They had a room in an inn on St. Lawrence Street, and from the window Marie-Anne could see the tall masts of the many ships anchored in the harbour. She could also see the many warehouses with their gleaming metal roofs. When she asked Jean-Baptiste about them, he informed her they were to protect the buildings from fire. If a wood roof was used, the sparks from the many chimneys caused too many fires.

During the afternoon of the second day, Jean-Baptiste returned to their room with a smug look on his face as he informed Marie-Anne, "I'm sorry, Marie-Anne, but the brigade master says you can't come. There's no room for a passenger in the freight canoes, and all the express canoes have already left. You'll have to go back to Maskinonge."

"But I'm ready to go. I've bought clothes especially for the journey. I've changed my feminine clothes for the clothes of a voyageur—heavy trousers, warm shirts, knitted stockings, a leather coat. I must go. I'll speak to some one in greater authority. Who's the boss of this company?"

Jean-Baptiste groaned. Would his wife never give up this foolish idea? Yet he answered her question. "The chief director is Monsieur William McGillivray. But he's a hard man to see."

"I'll see him," Marie-Anne promised.

Marie-Anne was surprised at the small stature of the man who sat behind the large desk. His deep voice beckoned her forward. "So, you're Madame Lagimodiere. I must say you're persistent. What can I do for you, Madame?"

Marie-Anne was amazed that he spoke French so well. She had worried that she might have to deal through an interpreter so she was pleased to use her own language. "Sir, I want to accompany my husband to Fort Garry, but his brigade master won't allow me into his canoe."

His blue eyes twinkled, and a hint of a smile played around his mouth. "So you wish to become a voyageur?"

"If necessary, yes. But I believe you have all the men you need."

"You're right, Madame. But I can't let you go with the brigade. If something should happen to you, I'd feel guilty the rest of my life."

She smiled. She doubted this man would harbour guilty feelings about anyone. "You needn't worry, Sir. I can take care of myself."

CHAPTER THREE

THE GRAND JOURNEY

▼

Marie-Anne woke with a start. Although it was still dark, she wondered if she had overslept. No, she couldn't have. Jean-Baptiste, beside her, snored peacefully. It must be the excitement that had awakened her. Today was the day they would start their voyage, their grand voyage to the West. As she thought of it, her heart beat faster. She tried to recall all the thrilling stories Jean-Baptiste had told her about the trip—the devil-may-care voyageurs, the rapids to be shot, the exhausting portages, the early morning risings, and the joyful arrivals.

Jean-Baptiste stirred. As he rubbed the sleep from his eyes, she whispered, "Jean-Baptiste, it's time to get up. We mustn't be late for the departure."

He growled, "Why are you whispering? I'm awake."

The eastern sky was turning light grey when they hired a hansom cab to take them to the embarkation point at Lachine, a small village on the south shore of Montreal Island, reached by a well-travelled road that followed the shoreline. In the lightening dawn, Marie-Anne studied the landscape. Trees of many kinds clothed the hillsides to her right, and the river to her left roared as the waters of the St. Lawrence hurried to the sea far to the east. Soon the village came into sight; it was a conglomeration of buildings, most of them warehouses. The first group of buildings was military warehouses; she noticed the sentries marching back and forth on their ordered rounds. The next buildings were the warehouses of the various merchants who did business in Upper Canada and farther west.

They stopped before the warehouses of the North West Company. Jean-Baptiste, who had been dozing, roused himself and retrieved their two duffels, the maximum baggage they were allowed.

It was light now as the cab ride had taken the better part of two hours. Already there was a great bustle down by the shore. Five great heavy-laded canoes were drawn up on the shore, as they had been loaded the previous day. Jean-Baptiste carried their bags to the noisy group. The joking, laughter, and cursing ceased as they drew near. Although Marie-Anne was dressed in the garb of a voyageur, the men had heard that a woman was joining them on the trip to Fort Kaministikwia, so they were not sure how they should behave.

Jean-Baptiste drew Marie-Anne forward. "Gentlemen, this is my wife, Marie-Anne." There were murmured greetings, but she wasn't sure of the men's attitude. Some seemed friendly enough, but others seemed resentful. That might be that they were shy, she thought.

Little time was spent in frivolity. The men pushed the heavy canoes with their five ton cargoes into the water and climbed aboard. Each of the five canoes had a crew of ten men—a man at the bow, and another at the stern, and four paddlers along each side. In Jean-Baptiste's canoe a place was found for Marie-Anne near the stern as that offered the driest ride. With a great shout the brigade was off.

Marie-Anne watched in wonder as the canoes followed the north shore of Lake St. Louis which was really a widening of the St. Lawrence River.

On the lake, as well, were several fleets of bateaux, flat-bottomed boats narrow at each end and propelled by long oars. She noticed they were the same length and width as the canoes, but they were manned by a much smaller crew—a steersman and four oarsmen. Jean-Baptiste told her they would follow the St. Lawrence River upstream to Upper Canada while their canoes would take the Ottawa or Grand River, as the old-timers called it, to Lake Huron.

The crews of the canoes bent their backs to the paddles as they worked against the strong current. Their first stop was the village of Ste. Anne, where they would stop for their first meal. Mass would be said for them in the tiny church: they would be blessed, and the priest would pray for their safety on the long and hazardous trip to the fur country.

Marie-Anne looked forward to the stop and the ceremony. Her treasured rosary was in her pocket, and she planned to have it blessed especially for the trip.

The sun was high in the sky when the brigade pulled into shore at Ste. Anne. The rugged voyageurs filed piously into the small frame church and solemnly waited their turn to confess their sins to the lone priest who awaited them in the confessional box, a structure at the back of the church with three connected cubicles—one for the priest in the centre and two smaller ones for the sinners on each side. Each man took his turn in the side cubicles to tell his sins through the grillwork of a small window with a shutter that the priest opened and closed as he listened to each man's confession. As many of these men had spent their winter in riotous living, there were many sins to be absolved.

Mass followed, and each received the small wafer that to him was the body and blood of Jesus Christ. Marie-Anne joined the men and reverently prayed that Ste. Anne, the mother of the blessed Mary, would watch over Jean-Baptiste and her and all the others on their journey to the West. The priest, at her request, blessed the rosary she presented to him.

Immediately after the ceremony fires were lit, and the men prepared a substantial meal of food they would not see on the trail—fresh meat, vegetables, bread, tea with great amounts of sugar, and rich pastries. For the next weeks their diet would consist of dried peas, salt pork, and hard biscuits. There was much laughter, joking, and singing. They had cleansed their souls; they were at peace with God and the world.

Soon it was time to leave, and now the real work of the trip would begin. The old-timers did not call the Ottawa the Grand River without reason—it was wide and swift with many difficult stretches before they arrived at its tributary, the Mattawa, more than two hundred miles upstream. The first part of their journey was easy as the river widened into the Lake of Two Mountains.

Marie-Anne marvelled at the strength and endurance of the short, stocky voyageurs. They paddled without break for an hour; then they took a short rest as they smoked a pipe of evil smelling tobacco before they set off again. This they continued until dark when they searched the banks of the river for a suitable spot to spend the night. Usually they had a special place in mind, one that had been used by many brigades before them.

The first day on the river was interesting for Marie-Anne. Everything was new and exciting, and fortunately the weather was pleasant. That night was spent at a campsite which had been used for over a hundred years: first by the Ottawa Indians when they were the main traders with other tribes, and then by the French who replaced the Indians, and now by the Nor'Westers who traded as far away as Lake Athabaska in the great Northwest. Not far from their campsite was a new settlement of a few years, Wrightstown—a settlement started by an American, Philemon Wright.

After a large meal, the men found a spot on the ground that might be comfortable and rolled up in their blankets. Soon the fires burned low and the snores of the exhausted men mingled with the night noises.

Marie-Anne could not sleep although she felt tired. The excitement of the day still possessed her; she tossed and turned as she reviewed the events of the day. Here she was in the wilderness with a group of rough men, heading into a future that was uncertain. Had she been foolish to leave her family and friends to follow her venturous husband? Would she live to regret her decision?

The night sounds soothed her: the rippling waters of the nearby river, the sighing wind in the trees overhead, the owl's hoot from the woods, and the scurrying of foraging small animals in the darkness. She felt at peace with herself, happy that her husband was nearby; finally sleep overtook her.

The next three weeks passed quickly as one day merged into the next. Without mishap the brigade made its way up the Ottawa to the Mattawa into Lake Talon and, after a short strenuous paddle, into Trout Lake. Then there was a short portage to Lake Nipissing. Here, the men gave a great shout for now they would be paddling with the current rather than against it. The trip down the French River was fast; soon they could see the great expanse of Lake Huron.

The fine weather continued, and they made good progress along the north shore of Lake Huron. One evening as Jean-Baptiste and she sat by their campfire, he glanced up from his tin plate of dried peas and salt pork and said, "Soon, Marie-Anne, we'll be at Sault Ste. Marie. Then you'll be able to sleep in a comfortable bed and even have a warm bath. The company has a fine trading post there, and there are other independent traders living there as well."

"Oh, that'll be nice. I'm looking forward to that."

"Yes, and that's almost the mid-point of our journey. I must say the weather's been very good. I hope it continues to be nice, especially when we're travelling on Lake Superior. It's such a large lake, it's almost like the ocean, so if there are storms, they're dangerous for our canoes."

"Are there any French women at Sault Ste. Marie?"

"No, my dear, you've seen the last white women for a long time. You're the first, my love."

He was proud of Marie-Anne. She had stood up under the gruelling pace and the trying conditions. Her face still glowed although there were signs of the many insects that had attacked her, especially the black flies and mosquitoes which were now in season. Her face was tanned so dark that she could pass for a native woman if it were not for her hair. The wind and sun had bleached it a lighter colour than it usually was—and it suited her. He thought she looked more beautiful than ever.

He was happy the men had accepted her and treated her with respect. They admired her patience and courage. Even when the going was rough, she never complained and did everything she could to make life easier.

Jean-Baptiste, as were all the men, looked forward to the short break and rest they would get at Sault Ste. Marie. The lock, which the company had built, would make the portage around the falls easy, and then they would have clear sailing on Lake Superior—no more unfavourable currents, just wind, sometimes favourable, sometimes tempests and storms.

"How long before we arrive, Jean-Baptiste?"

He shrugged noncommittally. One did not try to guess at these things. If all went well, it might be a matter of a few days, but if all went badly, then it might be a matter of a few weeks.

"Don't worry about it, Marie-Anne. We'll arrive when we get there." He laughed.

"What kind of an answer is that?"

"That's an Indian answer. You can't change what's about to happen. Be patient, and let God look after such things. He'll take care of us."

Two days later, on July 14, a Monday, they arrived at the post at Sault Ste. Marie. Although the location had been used for a long time as a meeting place by the Indians and it had been a trading post for many years, the present fort had been built by the North West Company in 1783. It was still an important place. The company fort was palisaded, and all its buildings were within the walls. As well, there were many buildings outside the enclosure—some belonging to independent traders and hunters, some the shacks of the local Chippeway or Ojibway Indians.

Once they entered the Ste. Marie River with its strong current and many islands, Marie-Anne knew they would soon be approaching 'civilization', and the idea excited her. She noticed the voyageurs plied their paddles with greater vigour, anticipating the coming rest. Jean-Baptiste had told her the night before that they would probably rest at 'the Sault' for a day or two before they challenged the great inland sea, Lake Superior.

When they rounded a bend in the river and the fort came into sight, a great cheer went up from the canoes. She shouted to Jean-Baptiste, "We're here. What a fine sight!"

Jean-Baptiste grinned at her but did not miss a stroke of his paddle. There was little doubt he was ready for a break.

The break was short. Two days later, they portaged, with the help of the company lock, around the falls that gave the fort its name, for 'sault' in French meant 'falls'.

Marie-Anne was awed by the expanse of the great lake whose south shore she could not see. It stretched into the distance like a great ocean. The waves came rolling in from the south-west in long swells, and the heavily-laden canoes wallowed through them, with what seemed, no progress. She noticed that the brigade stayed close to the north shore. The men were fresh and paddled with enthusiasm. Since there were no more portages until they reached Fort Kamistikwia or Fort William—for they had learned that the fort was to be renamed in honour of William McGillivray, the chief director of the company and the man that she had seen for permission to come on this brigade—the men were willing to apply their energies to the paddles.

The third day out the skies turned a leaden gray, and the winds shifted to the northwest. By mid-day the wind increased in force, and a pelting rain forced the voyageurs to exert themselves to the utmost. The sharp wind created jagged, steep waves, and the crews worked hard to keep their crafts facing into the wind.

Marie-Anne wondered why they didn't make for shore and wait until the weather was more favourable.

She shouted to Jean-Baptiste, "Why don't we go to shore and wait until the wind dies down?"

A look of annoyance crossed his face, and he shouted back, "What do you think we're trying to do?"

For a moment she stared at him, unbelieving. Then she realized that the strong wind was actually pushing them out into the lake. Fear gripped her. If the storm worsened, they would be driven further and further from shore. She looked ahead trying to find the shore. But there was no shore in sight. Nothing but swirling water. The waves were getting bigger; one moment their canoe was riding the crest, and Marie-Anne was sure it would break in two; the next moment they were in a valley surrounded by a wall of water. As they rose to the crest of a wave, Marie-Anne looked around to see how the other canoes were faring. She could see only two canoes, and the men were working desperately to keep their crafts headed into the wind.

The seriousness of the situation struck her. If a canoe swamped, there was no way the men and cargo could be saved for the other canoes could hardly look after itself. She raised her eyes to heaven and implored, "Jesus, Mary, Joseph, save us." Then she dug into her pocket and clasped her rosary reassuringly. Her fingers found the cross, and her lips moved in silent prayer. As her fingers grasped each bead and the prayers flowed from her lips, she felt calm descend upon her; she was sure they would safely ride out the storm. The minutes turned into hours; the men laboured on.

Darkness descended and still the man struggled to bring the canoe to shore. The night was black; they had no idea in which direction they were headed. They kept the wind in their face, and Marie-Anne prayed on, her eyes closed with fear. Gradually the wind abated, and the clouds that hid the stars broke up. The steersman located the North Star and knew in which direction to travel. The waves calmed and the canoe made headway. In the darkness, Marie-Anne could not see the four other canoes. She listened, but she could not hear them either.

After what seemed like hours, they found a quiet cove and a sandy beach where, by the light of the moon, they made camp. Soon two other canoes joined them, but two remained missing. The exhausted men lit fires, prepared a quick meal, and then crawled into their bedrolls. Although Marie-Anne had not paddled, she felt tired also; the fear and tension had exhausted her.

The early morning cry, "Leve, leve"—"Awake, awake,"—found her fatigued and unwilling to wake up. The brigade master was anxious to find the other canoes. He had built a large fire to act as a beacon, and he had placed leaves and grass on it so a large column of smoke rose into the still air. The skies were clear, the wind had subsided, the waves were now gentle ripples—it was a pleasant day.

Within an hour, a fourth canoe joined them. They waited another hour in hope that the last canoe would rendezvous with them, but it did not. Finally the brigade, minus the fifth canoe, got underway. Marie-Anne wondered about its fate. She asked Jean-Baptiste, "What do you think has happened to them?"

He frowned. "I'm not sure, but it's possible they got to shore further along. They'll meet up with us…or join another brigade…or…"

She understood the 'or'. She said a silent prayer for their safety or for their souls if God had decided otherwise. The party was subdued by the loss of one of their canoes; they seemed resigned to the possibility that their companions had drowned.

In the days that followed, their disappearance was accepted, and the men returned to their normal routine—rising early, paddling several hours, eating a hearty meal of peas or beans, salt pork, and sometimes dried biscuits or hurriedly cooked 'bannock', a kind of unleavened bread, and then paddling until sunset and the final meal of the day.

Each morning, Marie-Anne surveyed the landscape and sky to see if she could predict the weather for the day. She hoped they would never experience another storm on the great lake. The weather remained clear and calm; they made good time as they travelled ever westward.

Late one afternoon, the western skies darkened; huge clouds swept toward them and were upon them before they could reach the shore. Again the winds tore at them, the rain pelted them, and hail smashed against them. The waters swirled and roiled in fury. Terror seized Marie-Anne; she covered her head with the oilcloth cover that was used to protect the cargo. She didn't want to see the disappearance of another canoe.

Her fingers again worked her prayer beads, and she prayed fervently for God's protection.

The storm passed as quickly as it came. All the canoes safely weathered it. The men joined her in a prayer of thanksgiving.

The next day they arrived at Fort William on the Kaministikwia River. The new fort was impressive, but Jean-Baptiste said, "It's nothing like the fort at Grand Portage. It's too bad, it's on American soil. You know, Marie-Anne, that's why the Company had to move. The Americans insisted that they leave Grand Portage. They didn't want English traders in their territory. I suppose one day this fort will be as great as Grand Portage."

"Why is this such an important fort?"

"This is the place where the large "canots du maitre" are exchanged for the smaller "canots du Nord." In the North, most of the goods are transported by river rather than on the lakes…as well, the cargoes are smaller. Not too far from here is the divide, the place where the waters flow to the north and west, rather than south and east. When you pass that place, you'll be a true nor'wester."

"Is the country better than here?"

"Yes, especially the prairies, where the buffaloes roam."

They rested for two days, and then they were on their way again, this time with a larger brigade of ten smaller "canots du Nord." These canoes were on the average thirty feet long and carried a smaller load. There were more portages to make, particularly in the first part of the voyage. Up the Kaministikwia River to Dog Lake and up Dog River there were many portages. Marie-Anne felt sorry for the men as they carried two ninety pound pieces over the wet slippery trail. She found it hard going although she carried only her light duffel bag. Finally they arrived at Savanne Portage; this was the height of land where the waters now flowed west. This was where she became a Nor'wester.

For the next two days, she seemed to be forever getting out of or into the canoe. They passed through Lac des Milles Lacs to Pickerel Lake down the Maligne River into Lac La Croix then into Rainy Lake. Once through

Lake of the Woods they were on its outlet, the Winnipeg River, a wide swift-flowing stream with numerous rapids, falls, and cascades which the voyageurs shot with enjoyment.

Each time the canoe pitched and rolled and barrelled through the rapids, Marie-Anne grasped the sides in terror, and screamed as she prayed for the saints to preserve her; they seemed to listen for they escaped unscathed. One day the river widened, and the current became peaceful; the paddlers propelled their crafts the last miles to their destination, Fort Alexander, at the mouth of the river where it emptied into the large but shallow Lake Winnipeg. Here the brigades broke up and dispersed to various destinations in the north, south, and west.

The evening before the brigades left for their posting a great party was held in the main room of the fort. Marie-Anne had never seen one like it. After a huge meal, the men moved the tables to the walls, and on one were seated the musicians—fiddlers, pipers, and drummers. The music started and the dancers moved to the centre of the floor as lively jigs and reels were played almost continuously. The young Indian girls joined the voyageurs; their agility and stamina surprised and impressed her. Marie-Anne was very popular; she didn't miss a single dance the entire evening. Finally as the sun crept over the eastern horizon and the musicians refused to play any longer, the dancers dispersed and the party was over. This same day the tired voyageurs would be off to their lonely posts in the far reaches of the north, the west, and to the closer ones along the Red River and its tributary, the Assiniboine.

As they trudged wearily to their tent, Marie-Anne yawned. "I could sleep for a week."

"That won't be possible, my sweet. We leave this morning for the south. We're joining a brigade which is travelling to a fort called Pembina. It's a Hudson Bay post; I want to join the fall buffalo hunt. The Bay pays well for the pemmican we'll make."

She yawned again. "I'll be happy when we get there."

CHAPTER FOUR

A SERIOUS PROBLEM

▼

Marie-Anne stuck her head out of the canvas tent that was their home. The air was sharp and crisp; there was already a hint of Fall in the weather, but this morning in early September a pale pink glow diffused across the sky from the sun on the eastern horizon.

She turned to the interior and spoke to a mound of assorted blankets piled upon a thick buffalo robe. "Get up, lazy bones. There's no time to linger in bed on such a pleasant morning."

The blankets stirred and lunged at her. She moved away nimbly, speaking sharply, "Jean-Baptiste, it's late. There's much to do before we leave."

He spoke sadly. "Yes, that's true. And I must get away today if I want to join in the fall hunt."

"Oh, I wish you wouldn't go. I'll be so lonely. I don't know anyone."

"Don't worry. You'll see that the Indian women are very friendly. You'll have friends in no time. I've arranged for all your needs. Unfortunately, you'll have to live in the tent. There's no available space in the fort, and since I'm not an employee of the company I'm not entitled to any consideration, but the factor said he'd watch over you."

A frown wrinkle her brow. "Oh, I wish you didn't have to go. Or that I could go with you."

Jean-Baptiste sighed and said gently, "We've been over that. You're not ready to go on a buffalo hunt. You don't know how hard it is and how much work has to be done. No, you must stay here. You'd just be in the way if I brought you with me."

For a moment tears warmed her eyes, and she blinked several times to stop them. He was right. She knew nothing about the hunt, and even less about skinning and preparing the meat, and she wasn't sure she wanted to learn. Life was so different here than it had been in Maskinonge.

Finally she admitted, "You're right, but I'll be lonely and unhappy until you return." She smiled weakly. "Get up you lazy bones. It's time to get the fire going. I must cook breakfast. I'm hungry."

Soon Jean-Baptiste had a fire glowing in the ring of stones that was their fire-pit, and Marie-Anne bustled about preparing their morning meal which consisted of a gruel of pemmican, fish, Indian corn, and wild rice, the staple food of the western plains.

By the time the sun had risen and full daylight came to their campsite, she had washed their few dishes and put them away. Then she went about her own toilet. She vowed she would remain civilized—she would not become like the Indian women around her. She would wear the clothing of the East, dresses and petticoats, bonnets and gloves, shoes and stockings—these would be her attire. She wouldn't accept the cotton frock and the high vamped moccasins, and the braided hair of the Indian women. She was a white women; she was a Canadian.

Sometimes she was sure Jean-Baptiste disagreed with her ideas, but she planned to bring civilization to this wild land. He smiled, but said nothing.

As she combed her dark blonde hair, she realized it was getting long. She tied it at the back with a dark blue ribbon and surveyed her appearance in the shiny metal mirror hanging on the tent post. She'd have to get it cut. She ran her hands down the long skirt of her dress arranging it comfortably; then she turned to Jean-Baptiste who was watching her.

"You do look beautiful, my love. But I think you've put on a little weight. That dress seems a bit tight."

"You're right, but there's a good reason for that."

Jean-Baptiste looked at her quizzically. "I've been looking after you too well, my darling."

She wrinkled her nose and smiled broadly. "You don't know anything, my husband. Can't you see you're going to be a father?"

His eyes opened wide in surprise. He let out a whoop. "That's the best news I've heard in a long time. Me, Jean-Baptiste Lagimodiere, a father!"

The buffalo hunters had been gone only three days, yet Marie-Anne was lonely and miserable. There was very little for her to do around her camp except to prepare her meals and keep the tent tidy. Most of the time she sat thinking about the future. They couldn't live in the tent too long. Even now the nights were chilly, and on some mornings a light coating of frost covered the ground. Her baby wasn't due to arrive until sometime in the new year; she hoped that by then they would have their own house. It would never do to care for a new-born baby in a tent although she'd been told that the Indian women did it all the time.

She sat on a block of wood before the firepit staring into the dying coals. A shadow fell over her. Startled, she looked up into the darkest eyes she'd ever seen. Her heart lifted and her breathing quickened. Her hand went to her throat. A surprised "Oh!" escaped her lips.

The dark eyes were unsmiling, but her lips curved showing even, white teeth. The mouth moved. "Me friend. Me 'Prairie Crocus'."

For a moment Marie-Anne was speechless. The woman before her could speak French. Marie-Anne recovered her poise and smiled. "I'm Marie-Anne, wife of Jean-Baptiste Lagimodiere."

"Me know. You woman of 'The Great Hunter'."

Marie-Anne smiled. It wasn't the first time she'd heard her husband called 'The Great Hunter', and she was proud that he was so well respected.

"Me your friend. You lonesome without husband. Me alone too. All men gone to hunt buffalo."

Even though her French wasn't perfect, she was someone Marie-Anne could talk to. She rose, and was about to get another block of wood for a seat, but her uninvited guest squatted and sat cross-legged on the ground across the firepit from Marie-Anne.

Marie-Anne knew the Indians were addicted to tea so hospitality demanded she prepare a kettle of tea. She stirred the coals in the firepit and added several pieces of wood to them. In moments they burst into flames so she place a metal pot half-filled with water over them. Then she added a generous handful of tea to the water. Jean-Baptiste had taught her to make tea in the manner of the Northwest. Once it came to a boil, it was ready to serve.

Marie-Anne resumed her seat and looked over her guest. She appeared to be young—perhaps seventeen, but no more than eighteen. Her hair was shiny black, parted neatly in the centre and plaited into two long braids that hung down in front. The last six inches were interwoven with leather thongs and ended with beaded floral ornaments. Her brown face glistened as if it had been coated with oil or grease; it was smooth and unblemished. A dark brown knitted shawl tied at her neck covered her shoulders. She wore a bright figured shapeless dress that came below her knees while her feet and ankles were covered with tawny coloured moccasins with a beaded floral design. The tops came above her ankles and were held in place with leather laces that encircled her lower legs several times. Even seated, Marie-Anne could see that she was a robust girl.

The woman looked up at her and smiled. "Me you friend, you my friend."

Marie-Anne returned the smile. "Thank you. I'd like to be your friend. Where are you staying now?"

"My people have camp on other side of river. We stay there till hunt is over. Then we go trap beaver and muskrat."

"Oh. Where do you trap beaver and muskrats?"

"We go north on Lake Winnipeg. Many beaver lodges there. Many muskrat lodges also."

"Do you have a husband and family, Prairie Crocus?"

"Yes, I have man, but he gone now, he come back soon."

"Oh, he's away on the hunt?"

"Yes, he on hunt, but he come back to me when hunt is finished."

Marie-Anne smiled. This Indian woman was just like her: waiting for her husband to return after the fall hunt. They had much in common. Marie-Anne poured tea into two tin cups.

During the next two weeks her new-found friend, Prairie Crocus, came to visit almost every afternoon. Marie-Anne looked forward to these visits as it made the time pass more quickly. Although the conversation was limited because Marie-Anne could not speak the Indian woman's language, which was Cree, and the woman's command of French was not enough to carry on an animated discussion, they enjoyed each other's company.

Each visit, Marie-Anne prepared the strong, sweet tea that Prairie Crocus liked. Often they sat across from each other saying nothing, but at other times Marie-Anne tried to learn some words of her guest's language because she knew that Jean-Baptiste was not ready to return to Lower Canada and Maskinonge. If they were to live on the Red River then she would have to learn the language of the people as Jean-Baptiste had done.

Prairie Crocus did not talk about herself much. From what Marie-Anne could gather, this band of Indians came from farther north, in an area along the western shore of Lake Winnipeg, but they often came to the Pembina area to take part in the great buffalo hunt that took place every fall. Hundreds of Indians and Metis, and a few Canadians such as Jean-Baptiste, gathered at Pembina to seek out the great herds of buffalo that roamed the plains to the west.

These hunts were organized like a military operation. It was commanded by a hunt master chosen in a free vote by all the hunters. He then chose his captains from among the hunters who were chosen for their ability to command respect. After the captains had been chosen, the hunters grouped themselves with the captain they wished to command them.

Thus the entire camp was divided into companies of ten to twelve men under the absolute rule of the hunt master and his captains.

Then the women and children, particularly those who were old enough to help, followed the men, driving the ox and horse drawn two-wheeled Red River carts whose ungreased wheels could be heard squealing and screeching across the prairies. The hunters were mounted on the best horses, and each man usually had a string of two or three more.

All this Marie-Anne learned from Jean-Baptiste and Prairie Crocus who seemed to know a great deal about such things.

One afternoon as they sat before the glowing firepit talking about the hunt, Marie-Anne asked, "What do the women do on the hunt?"

"The important work," she grunted in disgust at Marie-Anne's ignorance.

"What's that?"

"They skin buffalo. They prepare meat."

Marie-Anne paused. She was embarrassed by her ignorance, but she wanted to know. "How?"

The Indian woman looked at her, scorn in her eyes. They seemed to say, "This white woman knows nothing," but she answered slowly, groping for the words. "The women and children find the dead animals. They take skin, tongue, nose. They make great feast. Everyone eat. Much laughing. Much singing. The hunt is good. Next day, much work. Meat is cut in strips. Dried over small fire. Pounded into pieces. Put with fat, berries, and into leather bags. Now pemmican. For winter food or sell or trade to companies."

Marie-Anne listened attentively, but she could not imagine the preparing of such meat out on the prairies.

She knew that most of the men and women of the post, and most of the Indians from the camp across the river had gone on the hunt so she wondered why Prairie Crocus had not gone. She asked, "Prairie Crocus, why aren't you on the hunt with your husband?"

The Indian woman's eyes narrowed; she seemed not to understand Marie-Anne's question. She stared at the white woman.

As Marie-Anne was about to repeat the question, she answered in a flat voice, "My man not want me on this hunt. But next time I go."

Marie-Anne was puzzled. It seemed that the women did a great deal of the work on the hunt. Theirs was an important job: preparing the meat after the hunters had killed the animals. Yet her husband had left her behind. Why?

Marie-Anne was about to ask, then decided against it.

The next Wednesday afternoon Marie-Anne went to the fort trading room to get more tea. The trading room was a large room with a counter along one side which divided it into two sections—a small anteroom and a large display and storage area where a clerk held domain. This area was packed: on the shelves that lined the walls were various boxes and bins of merchandise; on pegs and nails were other articles such as traps, snares, harnesses, saddles, and other things needed in the hunt.

When Marie-Anne entered, there was another customer waiting to be served. Marie-Anne recognized her as the Indian wife of one of the Canadians who worked for the Hudson's Bay Company and therefore lived within the post. Since Jean-Baptiste was an independent who worked for neither the Hudson's Bay Company or the North West Company: he was known as a "Freeman." The woman surveyed Marie-Anne from head to toe; then she smiled and said, "Good afternoon, Mrs. Lagimodiere. It's nice to meet you. My name's Moonshine, but my husband calls me Monique. I'm Mrs. Bellegarde."

"My name's Marie-Anne. It's nice to meet you, Monique."

The young clerk, a Scot, turned to Marie-Anne and in broken French with a mixture of Scottish burr said, "What can I do for you, Madame Lagimodiere?"

Marie-Anne placed her order and asked to have it put on her account. As with most customers, the company allowed them a credit which was settled periodically when the hunter, trapper, or trader exchanged his goods for the merchandise that he had received from the Company. Jean-Baptiste had such an account.

As she waited for her tea, she turned back to the Indian woman. "You must come to visit me at my camp, Monique. It would please me greatly."

The other woman smiled broadly, showing yellowed teeth and a dark spot where one of her upper teeth was missing. "I'd like that very much. When would be the best time?"

"Any afternoon. We could have tea together. Prairie Crocus from the band across the river visits often."

A shadow of annoyance crossed the woman's face. "I must see you soon. I'd prefer to see you when Prairie Crocus isn't there."

Marie-Anne was mystified. What was between the two women?

"Maybe I should come to see you?"

The woman beamed. "Yes, please do. Please come with me now. My house is across the courtyard."

Marie-Anne could think of no reason why she could not go, so she followed the woman across the main quadrangle of the post to one of the small, square-log buildings that was supplied to the married employees of the fort. The small building had one room: along the north wall was a small clay and stone fireplace; the west wall was lined with bunks—four; the south wall contained a single, small window and the door, while a small square table surrounded by four blocks of wood for seats lined the east wall. The room was cluttered with various pieces of clothing, and a saddle and several bridles hung from pegs on the wall. Two shelves over the table held several tin dishes and containers of tea and sugar.

A metal kettle hung from a hook over the smouldering fire in the fireplace, and a wisp of steam ascended from the hole in the cover where a handle had once been. Two swarthy children were asleep in the lower bunk near the window. They did not awaken when the women entered the room.

Monique pointed to them. "They're very tired. They didn't sleep well last night. The boy's Pierre, and the girl's Mathilde. He's almost three years old, and she's one year old."

Marie-Anne studied the children. They were dark and chubby with more of the Indian than the white man in their appearance. She patted her stomach. "I'll have a child in the new year. Jean-Baptiste is very happy. He's hoping for a son, but I'd like a daughter to keep me company when he's away."

The Indian woman frowned as if she had just remembered something unpleasant. As she bent over the kettle hanging in the fireplace, she spoke slowly, "Marie-Anne I've something important to tell you." She paused and stirred the coals. "Prairie Crocus isn't your friend. She's your enemy. She plans to kill you."

Marie-Anne's eyes opened wide in shock. Had she heard her new friend correctly? Why would she say such a thing? Was she jealous because Prairie Crocus was her friend? For several moments she was speechless. Then she asked, "How do you know this?"

The other woman looked unhappy. Her dark eyes were veiled. "She's my friend. She told me. I'm of the same band. She and I grew up together."

"Why does she want to kill me? I've done nothing to her." Marie-Anne could not believe that this women was telling her the truth. Prairie Crocus had been so friendly to her. She had come to visit her often. They enjoyed each other's company. It just could not be.

Monique rose slowly from her position before the fireplace. "Marie-Anne, Prairie Crocus is a very jealous person. You've taken Jean-Baptiste from her. She wanted to be his wife, but you're his woman now. She's never forgiven you for that so she decided to kill you, then she can have Jean-Baptiste again."

"But...but, Monique, how do you know this?"

"She's my friend. She told me what she planned to do. When the time is right, she'll poison you. She knows the kind of plants that will kill you quietly and silently."

"If you're her friend, why are you telling me this?"

"Because what she plans is wrong. I can't let my friend do something that's wrong. She won't listen to me, but if you know what she plans to do, you can stop her."

The next two weeks were tense for Marie-Anne. When Prairie Crocus came to visit, Marie-Anne never took her eyes off her. Even though Prairie Crocus acted as if nothing was amiss, and Marie-Anne wasn't sure that Monique had told her the truth, she waited anxiously for Jean-Baptiste to return.

On Wednesday of the first week of October the hunters returned. Marie-Anne was happy to see Jean-Baptiste. That evening as they sat around their campfire enjoying the good fall weather, she sat close to her husband his arm around her shoulders. For once in the past two weeks she felt safe.

Jean-Baptiste held her tightly. "Were you lonesome, my love?"

"Very. Oh, I'm so happy to see you." She twisted to face him. "I've something important to tell you."

He laughed. "I already know that we're going to have a child."

"No, it's not that. It's about an Indian girl I met. Prairie Crocus. Do you know her?"

A long pause followed. "Yes, I know her. She belongs to the Cree tribe, Red Fox's band. They were on the hunt with us. Why?"

Marie-Anne looked carefully at him. "She plans to kill me."

Jean-Baptiste frowned; a concerned look swept over his face. "How do you know that? Why would she want to kill you?"

Marie-Anne hesitated. Maybe it was only a story that Monique had made up. Maybe she was the one who was jealous and wanted Marie-Anne as her friend. "Jean-Baptiste, Monique Bellegarde told me. She told me that Prairie Crocus wants you as her husband. If she kills me she can have you. So she's planning to kill me."

He was silent for several moments, then he muttered, "She'll do it. She's a crafty one. She'll do it."

The worry in his voice frightened her. Now she was sure that it was true. What was she to do? What could they do?"

Jean-Baptiste took her by the shoulders and turned her to face him. Shock, worry, and fear glistened in his eyes. He spoke slowly and deliberately, "We must leave here. We must leave before that woman has a chance to harm you. If we stay here, there's no doubt in my mind that she'll try to kill you."

Jean-Baptiste's certainty did nothing to calm her. "But where will we go?"

He was silent for several minutes, deep in thought. Finally he spoke. "Soon Red Fox's band will leave for the winter trapping grounds. That's north along the shores of Lake Winnipeg. We must go south in the opposite direction. We'll go up the Pembina River. We'll stay there until there's no more danger. I'm sure that in a little while Prairie Crocus will forget me, and then there'll be no further danger. We must leave immediately. I'll work in the south."

CHAPTER FIVE

A BLESSED EVENT

▼

Marie-Anne wriggled beneath the heavy buffalo robe. She was warm and cozy; the thought of rising in the wintry dawn did not appeal to her. Jean-Baptiste lay beside her with his right arm around her. As she lay there snug and warm, she listened to the wind tearing at the canvas of their tent. The cloth flapped and the ceiling and walls billowed.

They had camped at this location since they hurriedly left the fort at Pembina almost three months before. The trip up the Pembina River had been uneventful, and Jean-Baptiste chose the location because it was well protected from the winter winds of the great plains that extended in every direction around them. He chose the mouth of a small creek that flowed into the slow moving Pembina River. Since there were a few trees along the banks to act as a windbreak and to provide firewood for their camp, he had decided to set up there.

During the past two and a half months, hunting had been good, and he had sold his game to trappers in the region who were busy trapping beavers and hunting for any other fur bearing animals. Winter was slowly descending upon the camp; although the temperature was cold, there was little snow, and the prairies looked barren and lonely.

Marie-Anne squirmed to face Jean-Baptiste. "Jean-Baptiste, don't you think it's time we thought of returning to Pembina. I'm sure there's no danger to me anymore. And soon it'll be time to have my baby."

In the past three months she had become large with child. She felt clumsy, and she found it difficult to do the chores around the camp. Jean-Baptiste would not let her haul the buckets of water from the creek to the camp, and he chided her when she lifted heavy things, but she felt strong and healthy and insisted on doing her share of the work. His job was to hunt and prepare the game that he shot; hers was to cook and keep the camp for him.

He smiled. "You know, Marie-Anne, I was thinking the same thing. I'm tired of hunting. We've enough money, and you're right. I don't think Prairie Crocus is a concern anymore. I'm sure she's far enough away. She probably has a husband by now."

"Oh, I'm happy. I didn't want to have my baby out on these cold prairies. When will we go back to Pembina?"

"Tomorrow. I'll find some poles to make a travois for the horse. That will carry our goods, and you can ride on it. I think you'll find that more comfortable than horseback."

Marie-Anne had seen many travois. A travois was two long poles that were tied together at one end and attached to a harness on the horse's back. The other ends of the poles dragged on the ground, and a few feet up from these ends was tied a sling that carried the baggage. She would sit atop the baggage. In winter, on the snow, it was almost like riding on a sleigh.

That day was a busy one as they prepared to break camp. All their goods had to be bundled and packaged and prepared so they could be packed aboard the travois. Together they worked to get their stuff ready.

They were fortunate for the weather was warm and pleasant. The sun shone brightly and the blue skies sparkled brilliantly. There was just enough snow on the frozen surface of the river to smooth out the ice surface. Marie-Anne was so happy that she sang most of the way. Since they were only twenty-five miles upriver from the fort, they arrived at Pembina late in the afternoon.

Marie-Anne couldn't remember when she had been so happy to see a place. The activity of the people at the fort enlivened her and she looked forward to renewing the friendships she had made. She wondered if Monique Bellegarde was still living within the fort. As they approached the open gate, Jean-Baptiste slowed the horse he was riding and brought it even with Marie-Anne perched on the travois. "I hope there's an empty house in the fort. I'll be able to rent it and we'll be more comfortable than in a tent."

Her heart leaped. That would be nice. She had not lived in a house since they left Montreal. On the trip she had lived under a turned-over canoe and here at Pembina she had lived in a tent as she had on the prairie. She was sure she would like even a small one room house such as the one Monique and Jean Bellegarde lived in. At least it would be warm.

One evening late in December, as Marie-Anne and Jean-Baptiste sat before a glowing fire in their small fireplace in the tiny log house that he had rented from the Hudson's Bay Company, he smiled at Marie-Anne and said, "It's pleasant to have a house for a change."

She beamed with pleasure. She was enjoying the small home they had acquired within the walls of the fort. It had become vacant because, during the winter, the company did not employ as many men as during the summer. The Lagimodieres rented it.

"Yes, it's very nice to live in a house again. It's nice to be with people again." She was referring to the Bellegardes who occupied the house next door. In the short time they had been in the fort, she and Monique had become friends. Marie-Anne was happy that Monique could speak French, and, as well, she was teaching Marie-Anne to speak Cree.

Jean-Baptiste reached over and took Marie-Anne's hand in his. "It's better that we're in the fort for the birth of our child."

Soon her baby would be born. She had worried that the child might be born in their lonesome camp far out on the prairies, but now she was relieved. At least there were people to help at the birth. The post even had a doctor if one was needed.

"Yes, I'm looking forward to that." She looked down at the tiny garment she was sewing. Since they had arrived back at Pembina a week before, she prepared garments for her expected child. She vowed that her child would not be treated like the native babies, wrapped in sphagnum moss and laced into a cradleboard which was hung from a convenient peg or slung over the mother's back."

Jean-Baptiste laughed at her. He pointed out how practical such an arrangement was: it didn't require many garments and the moss was an effective disposable diaper. She argued that she was bringing civilization to the West. Jean-Baptiste didn't argue. He was sure that time would show her the wisdom of the Indians' ways.

The next afternoon Monique came for tea carrying a cradleboard with a framework of willow branches and a pouch of beaded buckskin and moosehide. She handed it to Marie-Anne and smiled. "I want you to have this. My mother gave it to me for my children. I would like you to use it for your children."

Marie-Anne looked at her friend, and her heart filled with pleasure at the Indian woman's generosity. She reached for it. "Thank you, I'm sure I'll be able to use it," but her mind said, "I hoped that Jean-Baptiste would make a cradle like the one my mother used in Maskinonge." Her mind went back to her home in Maskinonge. What a difference there was between the people here and in Lower Canada! Most of the people here lived primitively. Only a few white men and their Indian wives and children lived in proper houses. The Indians lived in skin tents which they moved from place to place as they roamed about in search of food or the furs that they exchanged for food and other necessities—clothes and cloth, pots and pans, guns and traps.

The fort was quiet now as most of the Indians were far in the woods or out on the plains hunting and trapping, especially the beavers whose skins the traders of the two great companies and a few independents valued so highly.

Marie-Anne smiled and said, "Will Jean be back for the new year celebration?"

Monique shrugged her shoulders. "I think so. He always tries to be home for that."

Each year, to mark the beginning of the new year, the Hudson's Bay Company held a grand party. All its employees and their families were invited to a great banquet which was held in the largest room of the fort. After a meal of many dishes— most of them wild meat of various sorts— beaver, especially the tail; moose, especially the tongue and nose; deer; elk; rabbit; and ducks and geese of all kinds—and any vegetables that were available, usually potatoes and turnips that had been grown in the post garden—a lively dance was held. As the year came to an end, everyone anticipated this great party.

Marie-Anne listened attentively as people discussed it, and she looked forward to it as it would be her first. She hoped it would be as interesting as the one that was held at Fort Alexander when she first arrived in the country.

Marie-Anne looked down at the tiny bundle that lay beside her. Her heart overflowed with love. She twisted onto her side and slowly lifted the soft blanket that covered the child. This was her baby, her firstborn. The tiny pink face moved: the nose wrinkled, the mouth opened and closed, and the eyelids flickered as the child tried to open its eyes. Marie-Anne studied the child that just a short time ago had been part of her.

She looked up at Jean-Baptiste who sat on a block of wood a few feet away from her. She smiled wanly, and he reached over and took her hand in his. "She's a beautiful baby, Marie-Anne. She'll grow up to be admired by all men."

"No, Jean-Baptiste, she'll grow up to be the first nun from the West."

He smiled. He marvelled at his wife's faith. Even as she lay in her bed so shortly after having her baby, she was thinking of God and the Church. There was no church or priests in the West, but that did not prevent Marie-Anne from practising her religion.

"Oh, Jean-Baptiste, a daughter, just what I wanted. A daughter to keep me company when you're away hunting. I hope you're not too disappointed that she's not a son."

Jean-Bpatiste smiled. "I'm disappointed, but I'm sure the next one will be a boy."

Marie-Anne squeezed his hand.

"You must be tired, my love. I'll let you rest."

Monique, who had been standing in the shadows, spoke. "She's strong. Tomorrow she'll be up and about her work as usual. The baby's strong too. She'll be no problem."

Marie-Anne looked at her friend. "Thank you, Monique. I don't know what I'd have done without you. You were a great help."

"Yes, Monique, we're happy you were here. One day the young one will thank you herself."

Monique shrugged her shoulders as if the birth of a child was a matter of small concern.

Marie-Anne repeated, "Thank you, Monique." She turned to the child. Again she lifted the blanket and stared at her child. She studied the baby carefully. The child's head was hairless; a wisp of fine fuzz like the down from a young bird, light and almost invisible, made her look bald. She had a round face with pink, velvety cheeks. Her small nose wrinkled and her tiny nostrils, pink and moist, quivered as she breathed. Her deep red, heart-shaped lips wriggled as she slept peacefully. Her eyes were closed so Marie-Anne could not see their colour. She hoped they were blue like Jean-Baptiste's and not grey like hers. She took one of the tiny hands in hers and felt its warm smoothness. The tiny fingers curled around her finger, and a feeling of bliss and happiness enveloped her. God had created a new life, and she had helped in that creation.

She must do her utmost to raise the child as a child of God. She thought how difficult that would be if they stayed in this wild and primitive country. And it seemed that Jean-Baptiste had no intention—at least not at the present—of returning to Canada. He liked the freedom and lack of restraint in this country. One was free to move wherever he wished. There were no laws to impede him. If he treated the people about him well and did not favour either of the fur companies, he could do what he liked. These thoughts of the future flashed through her mind—hers and the child's.

Jean-Baptiste's voice startled her. "My love, have you thought of a name for the child?"

She had thought of many. If it had been a boy that would not be a problem. She would call him Jean-Baptiste, after his father. But the child was a girl, a beautiful girl. She must have a beautiful name.

"What day is it today?" she asked. She had lost track of time. The birth of her child made her forget the passage of time.

"Why, it's January 6, 1807," Jean-Baptiste answered.

"It's the feast of the Epiphany, the day the three wise kings came to the baby Jesus bearing gifts. Oh, it's so nice our daughter was born on this great feast day. That shows that God is watching over her. She will be our gift to him. The kings came to him and she came to us. We'll call her Renee. You know it means queen...'Reine'." She smiled, satisfied.

Marie-Anne was, as Monique stated, strong and healthy, and in two days she was back to her old self—almost. Jean-Baptiste noticed a change. She seemed more serious, and often there was a concerned look on her face. He was mystified: the child was serene and satisfied, and slept most of the time. She seldom cried or fussed; she didn't even disrupt their sleep much. But Marie-Anne seemed unhappy. After a week, Jean-Baptiste could stand it no longer.

"Marie-Anne, something's bothering you. What is it?"

She looked solemnly at him, but she said nothing. That, too, was not like her.

"Have I done something to displease you?"

She glanced at the child then looked back at him. "No, you've done nothing. I've been thinking about our life and the child's future."

"What do you mean, Marie-Anne? Is there something wrong with the child? Is something lacking? What is it that you need? Isn't there enough food?...or clothing?...or warmth, or love?" The last he added quickly.

"No, it's not that. The child has almost everything she needs."

He noticed the "almost". "You say 'almost'. What's missing?"

She stared at him for several moments. What is the matter with my husband that he can't see what's missing? "Jean-Baptiste, the most important thing is missing. The child will miss her relatives. No one has come to visit us and make a fuss over our new child. If we were back in Maskinonge, my parents and yours would come to congratulate us. They would look at the child; they would compliment us and her. They would say, 'What a beautiful child she is!' and they would even give her some small gifts—but here she is just another little animal to be fed and clothed and trained so she can grow up to work."

Jean-Baptiste wrinkled his brow. What she said was true, but that did not mean that she was missing love. He and her mother loved the child dearly. Was his wife trying to persuade him to return to Lower Canada?

"My dear, life here isn't much different from back home. In many ways it's easier—it's easier to make a living: food's easy to obtain, clothing and shelter, we can obtain from nature—the animals, the trees, the waters. And one is free to do what he pleases. The child will grow up strong and free."

"But she'll be a pagan. There are no priests; there is no church. She'll never know God...or the baby Jesus...or the blessed Mary...or Saint Joseph." Tears came to her eyes. If the child died suddenly, she would be damned forever. "That's what she'll miss. She'll miss religion."

"Life is changing in the West, Marie-Anne. Soon there'll be priests and churches here. You're the first Canadian woman to come west, but I'm sure you'll not be the last. Then when the priests come, nuns won't be far behind, and then there'll be schools."

"But that may be too late for our little Reine."

He frowned. He had to admit that that was possible.

She continued, "She hasn't been baptized. She doesn't even have a name yet. What'll we do?"

He noticed the quaver in her voice, and it made him feel guilty. "We'll register her with the Company."

"You see, Jean-Baptiste, she's like a little animal. No one cares that she was born."

He realized the truth of her statement. It was true. The birth of native or Metis children was seldom recorded unless the woman was the wife of an important man in the Hudson's Bay Company or in the North West Company, and even then these men might forget their mixed-blood children. What were they to do?

"We mustn't let that happen to our child. We must have her birth recorded, and she must be baptized."

"You're right, Marie-Anne. It must be done. But how can we do it?"

"Jean-Baptiste, you must get the factor to record the birth in the post diary—the journal. But who'll baptize the child?'

Jean-Baptiste looked at his wife. "We will."

Marie-Anne's face broke into a smile.

Jean-Baptiste's face mirrored hers. He was happy that his wife would again be her joyful self.

They decided they would baptize the child on the following Sunday. They would make it a special day; they would invite their friends, and after the ceremony they would have a feast.

Sunday, January 25, 1807 was a cold, clear day. The sun shone brightly but there were ice crystal in the air and the temperature remained far below freezing. Everything was covered with hoar frost, giving the landscape the appearance of a fairyland.

During the past week Marie-Anne had been vital and vibrant as she bustled about the tiny cabin preparing foods for the celebration feast.

Jean-Baptiste had been busy also. He had gone hunting and had returned with fresh meat: a fat buck mule deer, two plump beavers, and he traded some meat for two young Canada geese.

He convinced the post factor to record Renee's birth in the company books, which pleased Marie-Anne as somehow that made the birth legal. They decided that Marie-Anne would perform the ceremony as she knew how to do it from her experience as housekeeper for the priest at Maskinonge.

The appointed time arrived and with it the invited guests—Monique and Jean Bellegarde and their two children, and two other families: the Challifoux and the Paquins, and their children. They were Canadians also who had married Indian women. They and Jean-Baptiste often worked together, hunting, trapping, and trading. The Challifoux had three children: the eldest was seven years old and the youngest was two—two boys and a girl, in that order. The Paquins had two children, a boy of five and a girl of three.

When all assembled, the tiny cabin was overcrowded and warm. Marie-Anne and Jean-Baptiste had arranged seating around the perimeter of the room, but most sat on the floor because that was their habit. In the centre of the room was a small table with a copper pot on it; beside it was a tin cup half-filled with water.

When everyone was seated and the children had been shushed, Marie-Anne took Renee who was wrapped in a single simple blanket and placed her in her husband's arms. The light from the single window glinted off the child's light golden fuzz and formed a halo around her head. Marie-Anne glanced at the child, then at Jean-Baptiste. The child looked like an angel, filling her heart with excitement.

She looked up at the encircling group. "Thank you for coming to share this day with us. Today our little girl will become a child of God. And she will have her name forever."

Jean-Baptiste smiled proudly. At his daughter and then his wife. His chest swelled. He was impressed with the way his wife was handling this solemn moment.

"Today we are gathered to baptize a child. To cleanse her from the sin of our first parents—Adam and Eve. We are opening the door of heaven to her."

All was hushed, and adults and children listened attentively. None had seen an event like this.

Marie-Anne motioned Jean-Baptiste to the table. She positioned the child so that her head was over the copper pot. Then she had him turn the child's head to face her.

"Now I will baptize her."

She took the tin cup and slowly poured the liquid over the child's forehead. As the stream of water flowed gently, she intoned solemnly, "I baptize thee, Renee, in the name of the Father, the Son, and the Holy Ghost."

The cool water startled the child who wriggled her head, squeezed her eyes, and waved her tiny fists, but she did not cry.

The simplicity of the ceremony seemed to surprise those attending, and its brevity disappointed them. But they smiled and understood its importance to Marie-Anne. Her daughter was baptized and had a name.

CHAPTER SIX

A NEW ADVENTURE

▼

Marie-Anne watched as Jean-Baptiste started the fire. The mosquitoes, black flies, and other insects engulfed her and the five month old Renee. She waved her hands and struck at them without effect—the swarming clouds returned to attack any bare spot they could find. She muttered, half to herself, "Hurry up, Jean-Baptiste. Get that fire going before these flies eat us alive."

Renee fussed from the protection of the cradleboard that was one of the few things that Marie-Anne had adopted from the native people of the West. Marie-Anne looked out of place in the eastern clothes that she wore. Jean-Baptiste had tried to get her to wear the dress of the natives—a loose dress, moccasins, and a blanket or shawl—but Marie-Anne refused. She wore a fitted dress with a long skirt to the ankles, several petticoats, laced ankle-length leather shoes, a short coat, and, on her head, a bonnet with narrow brim around her face. She insisted she could not give up her Eastern ways, and Jean-Baptiste knew that it was useless to argue with her.

Soon, using a flint and steel, Jean-Baptiste had a smoky fire going as did the other members of the party—three other families: the Bellegardes, the Challifoux, and the Paquins.

Marie-Anne called across the narrow clearing they had chosen as a campsite, "Monique, how are the children handling the mosquitoes?"

"Not very well. I don't think I've ever seen the flies and mosquitoes so bad."

Jean-Marie, who was squatted beside the smoking fire, added, "And it's only May. You should see them in June and July."

Marie-Anne wrinkled her nose in distaste. "Do you mean to say they can get worse? I hope we're not around then."

He laughed. "They can get much worse, but I hope we'll be on the prairies by then. They're not as bad on the prairies."

Marie-Anne walked over to a nearby aspen tree that had been used by other parties that camped on the site and hung the cradleboard by its carrying strap. The cradleboard swung gently quieting the child in it.

By this time the four fires had been lit in the centre of the open area, and the men started raising the canvas tents that they had purchased from the North West Company at Fort Garry. The women busied themselves preparing the evening meal which consisted of pemmican stew, hard biscuits, and tea.

Jean-Baptiste, his mouth full of the nutritious stew, called to his friend, Jean Bellegarde, "Jean, in three days time we should arrive at Fort Cumberland. Maybe one of us should go ahead and see if there's any work there."

"That may be a good idea. Our supplies are running low. Whoever goes can live off the land."

"Maybe you and Ovid could go on, and Pierre and I'll travel with the women and children."

Jean-Baptiste was sure that Marie-Anne would never agree to let him go ahead without her. The other men, Ovid Paquin and Pierre Chalifoux, were married to Cree Indian women who were used to this kind of travel. The four families had left Pembina the first week in May and were hoping to reach Fort des Prairies, which was now located on the far reaches of the North Saskatchewan River, before fall. The men were independents or "freemen". They worked for any company that required their produce whether it was meat, pemmican, or furs. Jean-Baptiste had convinced them to join him and move further west as the trapping had fallen off around Pembina.

For the past three weeks they had travelled at a leisurely pace—down the Red River, along the west shore of the great Lake Winnipeg whose name meant "nasty or dirty waters" as it was very muddy.

This day they had portaged around the mighty Grand Rapids that introduced them to the potent Saskatchewan River at the point where it flowed into Lake Winnipeg. Now they were camped on the north shore of Cedar Lake.

Jean nodded his approval of the idea, and Ovid looked enthusiastic. It would give the men an opportunity to leave the women and squalling children and to meet some of their fellow voyageurs.

"Fine. Then you'll leave early tomorrow morning."

Marie-Anne was apprehensive about the trip. It was taking her further into the wilderness, not closer to civilization.

Four days later the two canoes, lightened by the departure of Jean Bellegarde and Ovid Paquin, arrived at Fort Cumberland. Jean and Ovid stood at the landing before the fort, a large group of Indians gathered behind them as a welcoming committee.

Marie-Anne, who was sitting with the children in the centre of the canoe, twisted toward Jean-Baptiste in the stern and said, "What's happening. Why are there so many people waiting our arrival?"

Jean-Baptiste smiled. "I suspect that Bellegarde has prepared for our arrival. No doubt they're waiting to see the first lady of the West. You know Jean. If he can make use of a situation, he will. I'm not sure what he's told the Indians about you, but I'm sure it's most interesting."

Monique, at the bow, turned and grinned mischievously at Marie-Anne. "I'm sure Jean has made you out to be some special queen, maybe even a goddess. So you'd better act properly."

As they approached the shore, Marie-Anne could see the serious, solemn faces of the gathered natives. Her heartbeat quickened. What was she to do? What did they expect of her? Why were they so unsmiling? What had Bellegarde told them about her?

Jean-Baptiste said, "Marie-Anne, be careful what you say. Don't offend these people. It's important we keep their friendship."

She thought, Oh, Jean-Baptiste, you're a great help. You make me feel it's my fault if something goes wrong. She said, "I'll try to do what's right. I hope they'll accept me."

Their canoe, which was in the lead, touched the sandy shore, and Bellegarde and Paquin came to bring it in. Bellegarde bowed at the waist and swept off his hat with a flourish. "Welcome to Fort Cumberland, fair goddess. Your humble servants await." He turned and indicated the assembled natives.

Marie-Anne scowled slightly. "What have you told these poor people, Jean?"

He laughed. "I told them you're a great white goddess, and if they treat you with honour, you wouldn't use your great powers against them."

Jean-Baptiste, who had stepped into the shallow water and was steadying the canoe, railed, "Jean, that was foolish. These people are very superstitious. They'll expect great things of Marie-Anne...and when she can't produce, they may turn ugly."

"Oh, don't worry so, Jean-Baptiste. See...they're ready to greet her with speeches and gifts. One must take advantage of these situations. The respect they have for her will only help us. You'll see."

Marie-Anne wished she felt the confidence Jean had.

At that moment, a tall, slim Indian dressed in buckskin leggings with a fringe down each side, beaded dark moosehide moccasins, and a dark blue coat trimmed with gold braid and a bright red lining, and a black felt hat with three feathers dangling from the crown, stepped forward. He bowed solemnly and handed Marie-Anne a pipe with a stone bowl and a long wooden stem decorated with a leather braid interwoven with various feathers and beads. A thin wisp of smoke drifted from the bowl, and the acrid smell irritated Marie-Anne's nose.

Jean-Baptiste whispered, "You must smoke it, Marie-Anne. Take it with two hands, lift it to the sun, and then take three long puffs. Whatever you do, don't cough or choke. That would be a sign of great disrespect to their god, the Great Manitou."

Marie-Anne stepped out of the canoe, Jean-Baptiste and Jean holding her by the hand on each side. She moved toward the Indian chief and extended both her hands. He placed the pipe gently into her hands. For several moments she stared at the pipe. Then she lifted it to the sun three times and placed the long stem into her mouth. She inhaled gently and drew some of the bitter, biting smoke into her mouth. The heat and pungent taste gagged her; she thought she would cough, but she quickly blew it out with a sharp puff. She licked her lips and repeated the procedure a second time and then a third time. She handed the pipe to the Indian.

He lifted it to the sun, drew on it three times, and handed it to another Indian who stood behind him in a costume as motley as his, though not quite as elaborate. The ceremony was repeated three times with three other men.

Behind her, Jean Bellegard whispered, "These chiefs aren't as important, but don't treat them with less dignity. One day they may be as important."

Marie-Anne smiled. She was enjoying her new-found importance. It was a pleasant feeling to be treated like a queen, even though she was sure it wouldn't last long. After the pipe smoking ceremony was finished, the first man stood before her, waved his hands to have his followers sit down, and then he spoke in Cree.

"Great White Lady, welcome to our land. We are glad that you have come among us. We know that you will look upon us with kindness, and that your presence will make the Great Manitou look on us with favour. Because you are here, the hunt will be favourable, the beavers will be plentiful, and all nature will be happy to have you with us."

Marie-Anne's command of the Cree language was still limited, but Jean-Baptiste knew it well so he translated for her. Marie-Anne smiled as she listened because she noticed the solemn faces of the crowd relaxed, and smiles came to their faces. Now she understood the serious aspect of the people: they feared her. Since she smiled, they believed that they had won her favour.

Four other speakers followed, and three of them came bearing gifts—a pair of beaded moccasins, a porcupine quill decorated belt, and a new cradle-board for Renee. She accepted each graciously and smiled her appreciation. Each time she smiled a murmur of approval passed through the throng.

After that the factor of the post came forward and officially welcomed her, the first white woman to visit the post. The Indians stared at her with respect as they saw how the Hudson Bay's man treated her. The remainder of the travellers followed slowly as Marie-Anne and her family made their way to the palisaded walls of the old fort.

"Welcome to Fort Cumberland, Madame Lagimodiere...the oldest Hudson Bay Company post in the Northwest."

Marie-Anne could understand no English so Jean-Baptiste interpreted for her.

The factor continued. "This fort was built in 1774 by Samuel Hearne as he explored this country...the Hudson's Bay Company has been here since. It was named after our great governor, Prince Rupert, who was the Duke of Cumberland. It's an important post as it's at the junction of the Churchill and Saskatchewan river routes. Bellegarde told me you and your party plan to travel to Forts des Prairies. Mr. James Bird's in charge there. You'll find him a very pleasant fellow."

The next five days were enjoyable for Marie-Anne. She, Jean-Baptiste, and Renee were guests of the post while the rest of the party camped outside the walls close to the area that was reserved for the Indians, and area known as the 'plantation'. Throughout their stay the Indians treated her with respect and honour. Each time she left the fort, the Indian children gathered around to touch her eastern clothes. Of particular fascination were her leather, heeled shoes. Mothers called apprehensively to their children; they feared the influence of her evil eye that Bellegarde had warned them about. He had told them that if they displeased her, she would look upon them, and they would be punished—they might even die.

The morning they left for the West, the entire fort and all the Indians camped nearby came to see them off. Marie-Anne turned to the crowd and said, "Thank you for your kindness and gifts, and may God bless all of you." She held her rosary aloft with the crucifix dangling. The Indians solemnly bowed their heads, and Jean-Baptiste whispered, "Don't overdo it. Sit down and let's be on our way."

"You're right, Jean-Baptiste. Let's be on our way."

They moved away from the shore; in the company of several other canoes manned by Indians who planned to escort them for a short way from the fort, they moved up stream.

Marie-Anne sat down and waved to the throng who returned her farewell. She wondered, Will I ever be treated as royally again? It's enjoyable to be treated like an important person, but it's also a great responsibility. These people believe I can plead for them to their god who'll make their lives more pleasant and enjoyable. Oh, that I could!

Their party had increased by one. Paul Bouvier, a Canadian who worked for the Hudson's Bay Company decided to join Jean-Baptiste and his friends to become a "freeman". He was a short, stocky, jovial man who was a great hit with the children. He always had a smile on his face and joke to bring a smile to others' faces. Marie-Anne found him a pleasant addition to their party.

The next two days, they journeyed in a leisurely manner. They were on the Saskatchewan River paddling westward. Although the east-flowing current was strong, they made good headway. There were no portages to hinder their progress. The second evening out they camped at the mouth of a river that flowed from the north into the Saskatchewan, the Torch River.

The July days were long with many hours of sunshine. The hours of darkness were few, and even then there was a slight glow on the eastern horizon. As Marie-Anne became more accustomed to the outdoor life, her enjoyment became greater. She learned how to cook efficiently over a small campfire, how to make use of the ever-present water of the rivers and streams to keep their meagre supply of clothes clean and fresh, and how to handle a paddle and to read the river. Each day she became more confident of her ability in the wilderness. She even learned how to use Jean-Baptiste's muzzle-loading, flintlock musket which was manufactured by Wheeler and Son of Birmingham, England and sold by the North West Company. She was proud that Jean-Baptiste was considered by everyone to be an expert marksman.

Darkness came slowly over their camp; the children had been put to bed, and the adults sat around the dying fires having a final cup of tea before they went to bed. Each family had its own camp and fire. Bouvier had chosen a spot to the north of the four tents and had erected a simple lean-to shelter as it appeared the weather would remain pleasant without rain.

Marie-Anne could see his silhouette hunched over the dying embers. She looked across their fire at Jean-Baptiste and remarked, "I'm happy Mr. Bouvier joined us. He's a pleasant man to travel with. Reine enjoys him very much. He makes her laugh whenever he plays with her."

"He's a fine fellow," Jean-Baptiste grunted.

There was a shriek from Bouvier and a dark hulk rose before him. In the shadowy dusk it was hard to see what was happening, but Jean-Baptiste, familiar with the wilderness, cried out, "A bear!"

A loud grunt came from the direction of Bouvier's camp, and a wild, high-pitched scream pierced the stillness. The sound of a scuffle and thrashing about made Marie-Anne's heart leap. She jumped to her feet and rushed to the tent where Renee lay sleeping. As she ran, she saw Jean-Baptiste grab his musket which was leaning against a nearby tree. She knew that he kept it ready, primed and loaded, for just such an emergency.

The grunting of the bear, the screaming of the man, and the thrashing about of the two made her shiver. Her mouth was dry and her throat was tight, choking her. The seconds ticked by like hours as she listened to the dreadful screams.

There was an explosion. Then a shriek. And silence.

Jean-Baptiste cried, "The bear is dead. I've shot him. I think Paul's dead too. Marie-Anne, come quick! Help me!"

Marie-Anne returned the child to her bed and hurried to join Jean-Baptiste. He pushed the bulk of the bear's body from the man who lay underneath. The bear was a large animal, and as Marie-Anne stooped to help her husband move the carcass, she felt warm moisture on her hands—blood. She wasn't sure if it was the bear's or the man's. Together they were able to free the man.

"Let's get him to the fire," Marie-Anne whispered hoarsely.

Jean-Baptiste grunted. Each grabbed an arm and dragged him slowly to their campfire. By this time the other men had thrown bark and kindling on the coals to produce light. The commotion of moments ago had turned to stunned silence. Marie-Anne cradled the man's head in her lap and stared unbelieving at the damaged face. She cried out, "Mother of God, his face is gone!"

Jean-Baptiste whispered, "But he's still breathing. He's still alive."

The next three weeks were trying for the travellers, but especially for Marie-Anne. She assumed responsibility for the injured man. The bear had clawed his face viciously, tearing off most of his nose and blinding both his eyes. As well, he had deep cuts on his arms and shoulders, some from the claws and others from the teeth.

The evening of the attack Marie-Anne washed, cleaned, and bandaged the man's wounds. Monique and the other women gathered herbs to protect his wounds from infection. The next day they remained in camp to care for the injured man. The bleeding stopped, and the fever, which had risen during the night, slowly subsided; he became clear-minded and was able to aid them as they cared for him. Marie-Anne realized there was nothing she could do about his sight because his eyes were too badly damaged, but she carefully replaced the torn tissue of his nose as best she could and hoped it would heal satisfactorily.

In the days that followed, Bouvier lay on the soft bundles of their cargo in the middle of the canoe; he stayed there throughout the day as he was very weak; the least movement made him moan in pain. Marie-Anne ministered to his needs, giving him drink and food, attending to his bandages, and reassuring him that he would survive. She prayed with him to help him overcome his disaster.

After a week, Bouvier seemed out of danger: his wounds were healing, his strength was returning, his fever subsided, he began to feed himself.

One morning as Jean-Baptiste and Marie-Anne loaded the canoe to depart, Marie-Anne asked Jean-Baptiste, "What will happen to the poor man now? He won't be able to work again. His sight is gone…the poor man."

"I don't know, Marie-Anne. He worked for the Hudson's Bay Company for many years. It's too bad he quit them to become a freeman. If he was still working for them, maybe they'd look after him." He shook his head.

"What are we to do with him? We can't look after him much longer."

"Well, when we get to Forts des Prairies, we'll see. Jim Bird, an old friend of mine, is in charge at the Hudson's Bay post, Fort Edmonton. Maybe he'll have some ideas. As it's now, we'll just take care of him and get him to the fort."

"I don't understand. You mention Fort Edmonton and Forts des Prairies. Are they together?"

"Forts des Prairies is actually two posts—Fort Augustus, the North West Company post and Fort Edmonton, the Hudson's Bay post. There's great competition between the two companies…for the trade in the West. That's good for the freemen. If one doesn't want our services, the other does. I've worked for Mr. Bird before, and Mr. Quesnel of the North West Company is a friend. We'll have no trouble there." He smiled with satisfaction.

Marie-Anne picked up Renee, now a healthy, chubby child, seven months old. She often rebelled at being confined to the cradleboard as she wished to be free to crawl about and investigate all the interesting things about her. She could sit by herself, and whenever possible Marie-Anne took her out of the enclosing pouch of the cradleboard and allowed her to play in the bottom of the canoe. Then she had to watch the child carefully so she would not crawl to the gunwale, drag herself up, and fall overboard.

"I'll be happy when we arrive. It'll be nice to be in a house again."

Jean-Baptiste frowned. "I hope there's room in one of the forts. If not, then we'll have to stay in the tent until I can build a small cabin."

"At least we won't have to break camp each morning and we won't be travelling every day."

"But, my dear, you'll be alone then. I'll have to be out hunting and trapping. Remember, we've travelled this far to make our fortune. I hope the trade'll be better here than on the Red River."

"Why's the trade so bad?"

"It has something to do with the wars in Europe. A Frenchman by the name of Napoleon is stopping the trade in furs. I don't understand it, but it seems that he won't allow English goods into Europe. So we can't sell our furs—they're stored and rotting in our warehouses."

CHAPTER SEVEN

THE WIDE PRAIRIES

▼

The mid-August days were already getting shorter; there was a chill in the early morning air as they broke camp and struck out early each morning. Jean-Baptiste was hurrying the group now. He was eager to arrive. And Marie-Anne did not complain either; she was tired of travelling. Several times they journeyed even though the weather was cool and rainy, but the afternoon they arrived the sun was shining, the air was warm, and the breezes were light.

When they rounded a large bend in the river and Marie-Anne saw the high palisades of the two posts located on the flats above the river, she whispered to herself, "What a beautiful sight!"

The forts stood out from the backdrop of the high hills behind them that were covered with trees—trees and bushes of all sorts, but mostly tall poplars and aspens with smaller pines and firs scattered throughout. As well, the white bark of a few birches added to the scene. Marie-Anne was impressed.

Slowly the two canoes approached the sandy bar that was used as a landing place. Several canoes were drawn up on the shore, some overturned to keep out the rain. As their canoe scraped its bottom, Jean-Baptiste jumped into the shallow water and pushed it onto the beach.

Then he let out a shrill cry of happiness. Their journey was ended. They had arrived.

Several people came down the trail that led up to the flat—several children, two Indian women, and three white men. One of the white men stepped forward, his right hand extended in greeting.

"If it isn't my old friend, Jean-Baptiste Lagimodiere. Welcome."

Jean-Baptiste grabbed the older man's hand and shook it vigorously as he clasped him around the shoulders. "Thank you, Jim. It's nice to see you again."

"I heard you were coming. And with a beautiful wife. Such news travels fast, my friend."

Jean-Baptiste grinned shyly. Then he turned to Marie-Anne. "This is my wife, Marie-Anne, and the child's name is Renee, but we call her Reine."

The swarthy older man bowed at the waist. "It's my pleasure, Madame. You're welcome to my humble residence, and I hope you'll enjoy our hospitality."

Marie-Anne was surprised at the fluency of his French, and it pleased her to hear her native tongue even though she was now quite fluent in the Cree language.

Slowly they made their way up the winding trail which led to the gate of the palisade. Marie-Anne noticed that the two trading posts were a short distance apart. Around the gate of each, several people loitered—some children, some Indian men and women, and a few white men. James Bird, the factor of the Hudson's Bay post, with Jean-Baptiste at his side, led the way. Marie-Anne followed carrying Renee. Paul Bouvier followed after the rest of the travellers aided by two men that Bird had assigned to help him.

Bird looked Jean-Baptiste over carefully. "You look well-fed, my friend. Your new wife has looked after you well."

"Yes, she has, and she's learning the ways of the West quickly. The other wives have taught her a great deal—how to camp, how to cook on the trail, even how to speak Cree…but she's a quick learner." He smiled with pride.

"You'll stay at the fort, Jean-Baptiste. I need a hunter of your ability. You'll work for me, not the other company."

Jean-Baptiste knew that he was referring to the North West Company. The competition between the two companies was keen, and in the past year it had become more intense. The Hudson's Bay Company had been founded in 1670 by a group of Englishmen who had been given a charter by the king of England with the right to trade in the land whose rivers drained into the Hudson Bay. For many years the company had been content to wait in their forts by the Hudson Bay for the Indians to come to them, and they had been successful, but the French from Montreal, and after the British had conquered New France in 1759, some Scottish merchants had sent their traders into the West, intercepting the Indians as they travelled to the Bay. Finally the English company was forced to follow suit. The result was that wherever there was a North West trading post, there was a Hudson's Bay post not too far away.

April sunshine flooded through the doorway of the small log house that the Lagimodieres called home since their arrival at Forts des Prairies. Marie-Anne was spring cleaning while Jean-Baptiste sat on the log step before the door watching the antics of fourteen month old Renee. She was a robust energetic child with light brown hair, a great contrast to the black hair of her native and Metis playmates. Her laughing grey eyes gleamed as she tussled with a young, long-legged puppy, one of the numerous dogs that roamed the fort compound. The swishing sounds of a corn broom vigorously wielded came through the open door.

Marie-Anne came to the door to shake the dust from the broom. Jean-Baptiste looked up at her and smiled. "There's much work for a woman at a fort. You're always busy. I think you need a change."

She looked at him quizzically. "Now, my good husband, what have you got in mind?" She knew he had something on his mind; he was a restless man who could not bear to be idle too long.

"I was just thinking that we've been here long enough. I've been making plans for the summer."

"Oh?…what have you got in mind? Another long trip, maybe back to the Red River?"

He cocked his head and looked at her. Was she serious or was she joking? "No, I wasn't thinking of going back. There are more opportunities for a freeman here. Trapping's good, and the buffalo are abundant just a few miles to the south. And there's a good market for pemmican. Jim's told me that he'll buy all the pemmican I can supply. So I think I'll go buffalo hunting for the summer."

"And you intend to leave me and Reine here?"

"No, I was hoping you'd join me. The other wives will be with us. They'll make the pemmican as we kill the buffalo. It'll be a good chance for you to learn how it's done."

"How'll we be travelling?"

"We'll be using horses. The canoes aren't good for hunting buffalo."

Marie-Anne made a face. She preferred travelling by canoe even though she was a capable rider. She found riding in a canoe more comfortable and less tiring.

"I know you prefer the canoe, but we must be practical."

Marie-Anne looked down at her stomach. She was expecting another baby.

She smiled. "Do you think the wee one will like riding horses?"

Jean-Baptiste winked at her. "Any son of Jean-Baptiste Lagimodiere will love riding horses."

He had decided that the new child would be a boy, and nothing could shake his conviction. Marie-Anne hoped he would not be disappointed. Jean-Baptiste was an accomplished horsemen. She knew that he preferred horseback riding to paddling a canoe throughout the day. As well he loved to chase buffalo on horseback. Many times he had told her of an exciting happening during a hunt.

The idea of camping on the plains excited her. The freedom to do as one pleased rather than the restriction of fort-life appealed to her. She would have only her small family to care for rather than her share of the work that was expected of her as an occupant of the fort. Renee was walking and running about on her own; she could feed herself; she could dress herself—she only needed help to tie the knots of the various fasteners of her clothes and moccasins. It might be a pleasant summer.

"When will we be leaving?" There was a lilt in her voice.

He smiled. That had been easier than he had thought. But then his wife always amazed him. She was ready to try any new adventure with enthusiasm and good humour. It surprised him to see how well she had adjusted to her life among the native women. She did everything they did: she had learned to cook as they did—over a campfire, in a fire pit, in a fireplace, and on an iron stove, when it was available; she made her own clothes, carefully sewing them by hand and—he smiled—still in the style of Lower Canada, with a tight bodice and a full skirt. And she still wore petticoats and underclothing unlike the native women. She now wore moccasins because all her shoes had worn out.

The summer days were long and full of sunshine. Life on the open plains was pleasant. Game was abundant and nutritious. Although the small group was very busy, the work was agreeable and satisfying. When the men found a herd and killed as many animals as the women were able to prepare into pemmican, they set up camp for several days, sometimes as long as two weeks.

She and her friend, Monique Bellegarde, worked well together while the children amused themselves with impromptu games.

One afternoon in mid-July, Marie-Anne glanced up from her place beside the small fire that was used to dry the strips of buffalo meat; a party of several horsemen was approaching the camp.

She called to Monique who was busy cutting a chunk of meat into thin strips. Startled, Monique looked up, and her eyes narrowed as she shaded them with her hand to see better. "It looks like a Cree war party. I don't like it."

"What do you think they want?"

"I don't know, but this is Blackfoot country. It can mean no good. They're looking for trouble."

"What'll we do?"

"You're white, Marie-Anne, so I don't think they'll bother you, but I'm afraid for the children, especially Reine. They may take a fancy to her. You can never tell with such a party. I'll take the children and hide in the woods over there." She pointed to her right.

They were camped on the crest of the banks of a small river, and in the valley along the banks were clumps of willows and aspen trees. Without waiting for a reply from Marie-Anne, she gathered her two children and Renee and hurried them down the bank and out of sight among the bushes.

As the group of riders came closer, Marie-Anne counted ten riders and another ten horses being trailed behind. It was a war party as she could see the painted faces and the weapons at the ready: bows and arrows, long lances decorated with coloured feathers, and a few muskets. Their dress was as varied as their weapons; some wore only breech clouts and moccasins, others wore leggings and coats while others wore a mix of Indians garments and white man's clothes. All, though, had painted faces.

As they neared, Marie-Anne' heart beat faster. A thin sheen of sweat covered her body. What was she to do? They would kill her, she was sure. She must be prepared to die.

She rushed into the tent. Her only protection was God. She found her rosary, knelt down, and prayed fervently. "God protect me. Forgive me my sins and save my family. I love you and I'm yours." She knew that her prayer was confused and rambling, but she was sure God would understand under the circumstances.

She heard the horsemen ride into the camp—the pawing of the horses, the rattle of weapons, the grunting and muttering of the men. Each sound increased her heartbeat. She prayed harder. She heard someone dismount;

muffled footsteps moved about the camp; then she heard the cloth rustle as the opening to the tent was lifted. She lifted her eyes toward heaven.

Minutes passed. She kept her eyes closed and her lips moved in fervent prayer. Any moment she feared would be her last.

She heard a deep voice say, "Who is this woman? What is she doing here?" It was in Cree and she understood the words well.

Another higher pitched voice answered, "She's a white woman"

"What is she doing here?"

Marie-Anne continued praying, her hands clasped.

The second voice replied, "I don't know, but I'll ask her." She was amazed when she was asked in French, "Madame, who are you? What are you doing here?"

She turned her pale and distraught face toward the man. She saw a medium built man carrying a long lance, his face painted, standing beside a tall, slim, hawk-nosed Indian with of tuft of feathers falling along the right side of his head. He stood erect with the appearance of one in authority.

Marie-Anne spoke quickly in French. "Who are you? You speak French?" Her voice trembled; she tried to hide it but could not.

The smaller man stepped forward. "My name's Theophile Letendre. I'm an adopted member of this Cree band. We won't harm you. Don't be afraid. My chief, Grey Wolf, will protect you."

Marie-Anne felt a bit relieved, but she did not feel safe with this band. They looked fierce and warlike; she felt helpless and at their mercy. Slowly the two men backed out of the tent opening and the flap dropped down. She held her rosary and prayed piously. She prayed for Jean-Baptiste, that he would return from the hunt and rescue her.

The hours dragged by as she prayed and the band controlled her campsite. She watched through the narrow slit of the door flap as they helped themselves to her supplies. They looked into their stock of buffalo hides and bags of pemmican and their other staples—flour, beans, peas, and raisins. She watched as the painted warriors help themselves to anything they pleased.

The afternoon shadows lengthened as the sun made its way to the western sky. She knew that soon Jean-Baptiste would be back from the hunt. Just before the sun started to dip over the western horizon, she saw the men gather and talk quietly but excitedly. They stood looking to the south, waving their arms, pointing and gesticulating with their weapons.

The band became silent. The tall slender chief stood with his hand half raised—a signal for silence and a gesture of greeting. From a distance, a voice rang out. "Marie-Anne, are you safe? Have you been harmed?"

She could not keep the excitement from her voice. "No, they haven't harmed me. I'm safe."

She watched through the open flap as her husband and his companion slowly and cautiously entered the camp. He held his right hand up in greeting and stopped before the tall chief. Marie-Anne listened as he spoke. "I am your friend. I am peaceful. My name is Jean-Baptiste. This is my camp and my woman."

The chief returned the greeting, but he did not smile. "I am Grey Wolf and these are my warriors. We are looking for Blackfoot and horses. We come in peace to your camp. Your woman has been kind to us."

Marie-Anne smiled crookedly. Oh, she'd been very kind to them. They'd taken what they wanted, and she'd been held like a captive—confined to her tent, too frightened to come out.

"I am happy to hear that, oh, great Grey Wolf. You are welcome to my camp, but I would ask you to move away because my wife is ill and tired."

"Oh, that is why your wife acted so queer. She spent most of the day on her knees in her tent as if she was talking to someone." He paused. "We will move."

And they did.

The summer passed quickly, and her experience with the Cree war party was soon forgotten as they followed the buffalo herds further and further south. One day in late August, Jean-Baptiste decided it was time to return to Forts des Prairies which made Marie-Anne happy as it was soon time for her second child to be born. She hoped it would be born at the fort.

Late one afternoon, their little caravan made its way slowly northward. The caravan consisted of Jean-Baptiste in the lead mounted on his best horse while Marie-Anne followed behind him on his favourite buffalo hunting horse. Renee was seated behind her as she was still too young to ride on the travois with the Bellegarde children. Behind Marie-Anne was their third horse dragging a travois which was loaded with their camp and the hides and meat that they had acquired. The Bellegardes' travois followed next, and behind it, Monique rode a horse that also carried full saddle bags. At the rear rode Jean Bellegarde ever ready to protect them from any attack.

They travelled slowly as they planned to hunt as they journeyed. Jean-Baptiste lifted his hand to signal a stop. He had sighted something. They stopped, and Jean came riding from the rear.

"What is it?"

"There's a buffalo herd just over that knoll." He pointed ahead. "Marie-Anne's horse tells me. He's used to hunting. Look how excited he is. He senses the hunt."

Marie-Anne was having difficulty controlling her horse—it danced and pawed the ground and waved its head about. Without warning it pranced around the two men who had dismounted. In great leaps it headed for the rise ahead. She pulled back on the single rope hackamore that was attached to the horse's lower jaw. But to no avail. The animal raced to the top of the hill. With her left hand she reached behind her and held firmly to the child, Renee, who cried out in fear. With her right hand she held the rope and searched desperately for the racing horse's flying mane.

As they came over the top of the hill, the horse plunged into the herd of dark brown, almost black, bulls who slowly gathered speed as they raced away from the danger that they saw. The horse selected one of the largest bulls, as it had been trained to do, and raced alongside.

Marie-Anne glanced down at the crazed animal. She was so close that she could see the rolling eyes and the puffs of steam blowing from its moist nostrils.

She shouted at the galloping horse, but that seemed to urge the animal on. She looked up over the dark sea that roared around her. The herd was densely packed; the animals were thundering madly in pursuit of the leaders. She was surrounded by a waving mass of bolting animals.

She had no time to be frightened, but she realized that one slip—if either she or Renee fell from the horse they would be mashed by the thundering hoofs. Her grip tightened more tightly to Renee and the horse's mane.

Great clouds of dust rose from the milling animals and choked her. She whispered a silent prayer as she wondered how they would escape from what seemed certain death. She knew that her only hope was to allow the horse its head. It would, she hoped, tire and find its way out of the herd.

Her attention was drawn to a large hulk that came up to her on her left. She glanced toward it. Her heart leaped.

It was Jean-Baptiste racing alongside. He reached over and grabbed the hackamore close to the horse's jaw; slowly he drew its head beside his leg. Then carefully he worked his way out of the herd.

Suddenly they were out of the main body of the herd; the mass of animals thinned out. The herd passed them by, and he brought the horses to a stop.

Marie-Anne leaped from the horse carrying Renee with her. She sank to the ground cradling the child in her arms. Jean-Baptiste leaped from his horse, and still holding the hackamore of the two lathered horses, he enclosed the females in his arms.

"Are you hurt?" His voice showed his concern.

She cleared her throat and replied hoarsely, "I don't think so. But we're badly frightened."

The child's cries turned to muffled sobs as she snuggled against her mother's bosom.

By this time, the rest of the party arrived, and Monique rushed to Marie-Anne. "Are you all right? Is the child all right?" She looked at Marie-Anne knowingly.

Marie-Anne understood her meaning. She wasn't referring to Renee but to the child she was soon expecting. She replied, "I think so."

Jean Bellegarde looked at her with admiration in his eyes. "That was a very good ride, Marie-Anne."

She smiled. "It's not the kind of ride I want to take again today."

They all laughed.

"We'll camp here for the night. That's enough excitement for one day," Jean-Baptiste stated. No one disagreed.

Soon they located a small stream and pitched camp for the night.

But it was not the end of the excitement for that day. Later that night, with the help of Monique, Marie-Anne gave birth to her second child—a sturdy, healthy boy, just as Jean-Baptiste had predicted when Renee was born.

Jean-Baptiste beamed when Monique informed him that he was the father of a new son.

CHAPTER EIGHT

THE REMARKABLE THEFT

▼

Spring in 1808 came to the prairies with a great urgency: the sun shone brightly day after day melting the snow quickly and encouraging the grass to carpet the earth with its greenery; the birds returned cheerful and happy, rushing about in their hurry to produce new families. The whole world was alive and stirring.

Jean-Baptiste felt the urge too. He had already left with his friends to follow the buffalo herds on the great plains, but he left Marie-Anne behind, comfortable and safe at Fort Augustus, the Hudson's Bay post, one of the two posts at Forts des Prairies. He felt it would be too difficult for her to follow him with two small children. Renee was just over two years old, and the new baby, whom they called "Laprairie", was nine months old. So Jean-Baptiste had arranged with his friend, Factor James Bird, for his family to live in one of the post houses within the fort.

Marie-Anne glanced out the small window of her log house into the fort compound. A number of people moved about the area going about the business of the fort. She noticed that the large double gates stood open; people were coming and going. Several Indians—men, women, and children—headed for the trade room in the large main building of the post where the actual trading was done. She watched as a man dressed in the leather leggings and vest of the Blackfoot tribe followed by two women wrapped in trade blankets that were worn as a cloak, and behind them two children about five and seven years old made their way to the trade room door.

She muttered to herself, "The Blackfoot are very early this year. The hunt must have been good."

She looked at the light brown-haired Renee who played on the floor with her baby brother. The boy was a chubby baby with rosy cheeks and a fair complexion. The lightness of his skin complemented his white hair that ringed his head with massed curls like a halo. The Indians marvelled at the child who was a stark contrast to their own children. All wanted to touch him, to hold him, believing he was a good omen.

"Reine, you play with your brother while I go to the river for some water."

Renee looked up at her mother with her large grey eyes and smiled. She had begun to talk and could understand all her mother told her. She replied, "Yes, Mama, I will."

Marie-Anne seized the two wooden buckets that sat on a low bench near the door, hurried out, and closed the door carefully behind her. She always felt uneasy when she had to leave the children to get water. It was several hundred feet to the river, and no matter how she tried, it seemed to take too long. Yet Renee, as young as she was, was able to look after her brother.

She hurried through the gate and followed the path down to the river. There were numerous Indians coming and going. Since this band had been camped at the fort for almost a week, it was common to see them about. As she met them, she nodded or grunted a greeting to those that noticed her. These were Blackfoot who had come to the forts early to avoid an encounter with their traditional enemy, the Cree, who were still hunting and trapping in the northern woods. The Blackfoot lands were south of the North Saskatchewan River on the southern prairies. Lately, Marie-Anne heard, there was bad blood between the two tribes due to horse-stealing raids that had taken place.

She thought of these things as she made her way to the water's edge. Several large stones were used as stepping stones to the deeper water where she could dip her buckets without stirring up the river silt. Carefully she stepped from one stone to another, dipped her buckets till they were almost full, and made her way back to shore. Then she hefted the buckets and slowly climbed the hill to the clearing before the fort. As she reached the crest, she met an Indian woman carrying a child under the folds of the trade blanket that covered her head and shoulders and fell in folds about her body. Marie-Anne nodded to her, but the woman averted her eyes and hurried on.

As she entered the gate, James Bird hurried across the compound toward her.

"Marie-Anne, where are your children?"

She looked at him, startled. "I left them in the house while I went to get water."

"How many times have I told you...Quick, check them!"

Marie-Anne set down the two buckets and cried, "Why? What's the matter, Jim?"

"I just saw an Indian woman leaving your house, and she was carrying a child. I thought nothing of it because I thought you were there, but.... Let's check the children."

With a cry of anguish, Marie-Anne turned and rushed to the door of her home. It was closed, but she could hear the sobbing of a child behind it. She opened it and rushed to the small girl who stood in the middle of the room, rubbing her tear-stained cheeks. "Mama, Mama, 'Prairie' gone."

Marie-Anne turned and looked at the factor. "You're right, Jim. Someone has stolen my baby."

Then she remembered the woman who was leaving the fort as she was returning. She recalled the blanket-clad figure and the way she had looked at Marie-Anne when Marie-Anne had greeted her.

She turned back to the sobbing child. "Don't cry, Reine. It's not your fault. You stay here while Mama goes after Laprairie."

"Quickly, Marie-Anne, we must get her before she can hide him."

She needed no further urging. She whirled through the door and dashed across the compound to the gate. Jim Bird followed close behind. Outside the gate, she stopped and looked to her right. The Blackfoot encampment was across the river, but the woman had turned west rather than east down the main path to the river.

Marie-Anne could see a figure in the distance following a footpath that also led to the river. She did not hesitate. She was sure that it was the woman who had taken her child. She started running as fast as she could. The woman ahead did not look back, and Marie-Anne hoped that she would not until Marie-Anne had shortened the gap between them.

She ran until she thought her lungs would burst, but the distance was narrowing. Then the woman ahead turned and saw her pursuer. She started to hurry, but with her burden, she could not run as fast as Marie-Anne. And Marie-Anne ran as one possessed. She was certain the woman had her baby.

The path now wound down the steep bank. Willows and bushes grew on either side of the trail obscuring the woman ahead of her. Marie-Anne hoped she could catch the woman before she got to the river's edge. If the woman managed to cross the river with the child and get to the encampment, Marie-Anne feared she might lose the child. Other members of the band would help the woman hide the child.

Her lungs burned, her legs felt leadened, but she forced herself to hurry. She ran down the steep path, stumbling and sliding, but she kept her balance, and finally, after what seemed an eternity, she came to the narrow, muddy beach that fronted the river.

The woman had disappeared.

Marie-Anne looked to her left, then to her right—nothing. There was nothing on the water—no canoe, no raft, no horse—nothing. Just the silty grey water gurgling on its way to the sea.

She froze, and listened—only the birds twittering, the leaves murmuring, and the waters rippling. Where had the woman gone?

She heard a sound. Faint, but unmistakable. It was the sound of a child laughing. She was facing the bank to the north, and the sound seemed to come from her left. Slowly she moved toward it. There was a clump of red-barked dogwood newly in leaf. She moved toward it. She looked behind it. A young woman crouched, clutching something beneath a dirty, smoke-smelling blanket.

Marie-Anne reached down, grasped the woman by the shoulders, and dragged her toward the small clearing at the end of the steep path. She could hear someone struggling down the bank. As she held the woman, James Bird came down the last few feet of the bank and joined her beside the woman.

Panting, he gasped, "I see you got her. Does she have the child?"

"I don't know. I think so."

James Bird shouted at the woman in Blackfoot, "Where's the boy?"

Marie-Anne tore at the blanket, pulling it away from the woman's body. The child grinned up at his mother and gurgled gleefully. Marie-Anne's face broke into a smile. "Thank God, the little fellow's safe," she muttered as she clasped him in her arms.

The days turned into weeks, the weeks, into months, and a new year came. Life at the fort was pleasant and busy. Her children grew and were happy, playing with the many children who lived in the forts—the children of Canadian men and Indian women and the Indian children from the camps that came and went, mostly Cree but occasionally the Blackfoot from the south.

The spring of 1809 was late, but when it came, it burst upon the western prairies like an explosion. The forts rocked with activity as the brigades of canoes to take the furs of the past winter east were prepared. After they had left, a quiet descended as the forts rested for the summer. Then Marie-Anne noticed Jean-Baptiste's restlessness. He roamed about the fort like a lost man until one bright morning in late May, he looked at

her with wistful eyes. "Marie-Anne, I'm going back to the prairies to hunt
the buffalo and make pemmican. Do you want to come?"

She wasn't surprised. She sensed that he was looking for some sort of
activity. She thought for a moment. Two summers before, she had accompanied him and his partners, and she had enjoyed the experience. It was a
change from the dull routine of the fort. Her children were older now and
would require less work. Renee was over three years old while Laprairie
was over eighteen months old.

"That would be a nice way to spend the summer. When will we leave?"

The next week they were on the trail to the southern prairies. They were
alone as Jean-Baptiste's friends had decided to try their luck further east. It
did not bother Marie-Anne; she enjoyed the chance to be alone with her
husband and children. They were headed for a place known as Buffalo Lake
because of the abundance of buffalo that fed around its shores. But now they
were camped on the banks of a river called the Battle River because of the
many battles fought on its banks between the Cree and the Blackfoot and
their allies—the Bloods, the Piegans, and the Sarcees.

One morning, Marie-Anne was startled by Jean-Baptiste's angry shout.
"Those damn Indians have stolen all my horses."

Horse-stealing was a favourite pastime of the Indian bands that roamed
the plains during the summer, and the Indians were unconcerned about
who owned them.

She hurried to his side. He held the leather hobbles that he attached to
the front feet of his horses. They kept the horses from roaming too far
away from camp. He raised the leather strap and pointed to where it had
been neatly cut.

"See, they've cut the hobbles and taken the horses." His voice grated
with anger. "I'll have to go after them. I know there's an encampment half
a day to the west."

"Do you think they've taken our horses?"

"It wouldn't surprise me."

It was a serious matter to be without horses on the prairies as they were the main means of transportation, and they were necessary to hunt the buffalo. Without them, Marie-Anne realized, they were almost helpless.

"I'll have to leave you and the children while I look for the horses."

She knew that had to be. She and the children would only hinder him. As it was, a man on foot was at a disadvantage; his progress would be slow. She watched as he set off at a quick pace, his musket slung over his shoulder.

She busied herself about the camp to keep her mind off the danger Jean-Baptiste might be in.

In mid-afternoon, before she noticed them, a large band of Indians surrounded her camp. Her heart leaped when she recognized them as Sarcees from the far south. They were painted and well armed so she knew they were a war party.

Marie-Anne glanced around looking for an escape route, but there was none. A sheen of sweat covered her body; she felt cold. Her stomach seemed caved in.

Their leader was a young, husky brave with dark flashing eyes. He rode up to her and demanded in a stern tone, "Where is your husband?"

She stared directly into his dark eyes, hiding her fear as best she could. "He's gone to get his horses that were stolen by the Cree."

He smiled broadly. "They're our enemy also. We've already killed one camp. We'll find this camp and help your husband get his horses."

Marie-Anne thought to herself, Then they'll take our horses. But she smiled instead and said, "It's late in the day and your warriors are tired. I'll prepare a feast and we'll smoke the peace pipe." She spoke slowly and evenly trying to still her pounding heart.

Marie-Anne had a good supply of meat, mostly pemmican, so she prepared a feast for the war party. She also had a small supply of tobacco which she divided among the young braves; then they smoked the peace pipe. As they were finishing the ceremony, Jean-Baptiste rode into camp with the stolen horses that he had retrieved from the Cree camp.

Although he was surprised to see such a small party so far north, he greeted the braves cordially.

The leader inquired, "Where is the Cree camp? We are hunting for Crees." His voice was angry.

"They're many days to the west. You'll not find them today." He knew of the enmity between the two tribes; he did not wish to aid either; he hoped to remain friendly with both.

"You are not Cree. We are your friends. We want Cree. We will kill the Cree. We have already killed many Cree women and children. We will kill more."

Marie-Anne wondered which camp they had attacked. Had it been some of her friends? Maybe these warriors were only bluffing? She did not feel comfortable with such a war-like party. She listened as Jean-Baptiste talked with them.

"You will lead us to the Cree camp tomorrow."

Jean-Baptiste shrugged his shoulders. He had little choice.

The brave continued, "After we have destroyed the Cree camp, we will go to the fort. Some of our friends are there—captives. You will help us free them."

"I'll help you if you'll let me camp away from your camp. My wife and children can't sleep. There's too much noise. Your warriors are too noisy. We'll sleep in that clump of trees over there." He pointed to a coppice of small aspen trees.

The brave stood silent, glaring at Jean-Baptiste. "If you try to escape we will cut off your heads. Do you understand?"

Jean-Baptiste nodded gravely. He didn't doubt the threat. He whispered to Marie-Anne, "When they're asleep, we'll flee to the fort."

They moved their tent and sleeping robes to the clump of trees and watched impatiently as the band settled in their camp. The hours passed slowly as Jean-Baptiste, Marie-Anne, and the children feigned sleep, waiting for the Indian camp to settle for the night. Finally, all seemed quiet; the camp had fallen asleep.

Jean-Baptiste whispered to Marie-Anne, "We must flee; we're not safe here. I'll sneak out, get two horses, and we'll ride as fast as we can to the fort. If we're lucky and get a good head start, we should beat them to the fort."

Marie-Anne's heart thumped so loudly that she was sure the Indians in the camp could hear it. She grasped his hand and squeezed it. "I hope you're right. They say they've already killed some women and children. Do you think that's true?"

"It wouldn't surprise me. This is a young party. They don't have an older chief to control them. Wait while I get the horses."

"I'll take the children to the next ravine and wait for you."

"That's a good idea. I'll find you there."

In a moment he was gone. She shook the children awake warning them to be very quiet. They seemed to sense the danger and followed her instructions exactly. In the darkness she made her way to the top of a rise to her left. Within minutes, Jean-Baptiste arrived with his two best horses—the other two he left behind. He set Renee in front of him; Marie-Anne had the boy in front of her. In the darkness, they made their way slowly northward until they were sure they were not being followed; then they urged their horses to a much faster gait.

Apprehensively, Marie-Anne glanced back at regular intervals, sometimes imagining she could hear the sounds of pursuers, but there were none. Throughout the night, they rode, stopping only occasionally to breathe the horses. As the summer sky brightened she made out the familiar landmarks that told her they were approaching the fort.

The longer they rode the more tired the children became, and they fussed and complained, but she knew they could not stop. By now, the war party knew they had been tricked and would not be far behind them. When they reached the North Saskatchewan River at a ford a few miles west of the fort, a great weight fell from her shoulders; they would arrive safely.

As they drew near, they were surprised to see that the gates of the forts were closed. Usually the gates were left open unless there was a possibility of attack from a marauding band of Indians. The tall pickets of the palisade looked formidable and secure. Marie-Anne felt that once they were inside the compound, they would be safe from the Sarcee war party.

They reined their horses in before the tall gates.

Jean-Baptiste shouted, "Will someone open the gate? We're being pursued by a war party."

From within came a voice. "Who is it? Who wants entry?"

"It's Jean-Baptiste Lagimodiere and his family. We're being pursued by a Sarcee war party. Let us in."

Slowly the tall gates creaked open, but only wide enough for a horse to pass through. Jean-Baptiste urged Marie-Anne forward with a wave of his hand; then he followed closely behind.

Pierre Chalifou and Jean Bellegarde, Jean-Baptiste's earlier partners, pushed the gates shut and dropped into place the heavy beams that locked the gates.

"Jean, what's going on? Why are the gates closed and barred?"

Jean-Baptiste jumped from his horse and lifted down his daughter. He handed the reins to the child and moved to help Marie-Anne dismount. First he took his blond, blue-eyed son and lifted him to the ground; then he helped his wife. The two men, his friends, came forward and took the reins of the tired horses.

Jean said, "My friend, it looks as if you've had a hard ride."

"We have. We're fleeing a band of young Sarcee warriors who were looking for trouble. They may not be far behind us."

"That must be the same band that caused us all our trouble." His eyes looked sad.

"What do you mean, Jean?" asked Marie-Anne. "What's happened? I thought you were hunting to the east."

"We were…until two days ago…but while Pierre and I were out hunting, this war party came upon our camp. They were looking for Cree." He stopped.

"Jean, Pierre, what happened?" Marie-Anne's voice shrilled with tension. "Where's Monique? The children?"

Jean shook his head.

Pierre looked down at the ground. He muttered, "They're gone. They're all gone."

Marie-Anne looked at him, unbelieving. Her face turned ashen. She gasped. "What do you mean? They're gone…they're gone where?"

Jean looked up to her face. "Monique and the children are dead. So are Pierre's woman and children." He rushed on. "They rode into camp while we were away…out hunting, and they killed. They just killed them. Because they were Cree…just because they were Cree." His voice quivered, and his eyes glistened.

Jean-Baptiste looked shocked and stunned. "Why? Why did they do that?"

Jean repeated, "Just because they were Cree."

For several moments there was silence. Then it was broken by gentle sobs as Marie-Anne mourned her friends.

CHAPTER NINE

BACK TO THE RED RIVER

▼

Marie-Anne studied her husband as he played with the sturdy Laprairie. The child was now two and a half years old, robust and active, and admired by all the Indians for his fair complexion, blond curls, and startling blue eyes. She knew that Jean-Baptiste was very proud of their son, but she also knew that he loved his daughters. Their third child had been born the summer before on the prairies far to the south in an area known as the Cypress Hills, so she affectionately called her 'Cypres', but officially she would be named 'Marie Josephte'.

She looked tenderly at the child as she slept in her cradleboard. She, like Marie-Anne's older children, was a satisfied, peaceful baby.

"Jean-Baptiste, our family's growing. Soon, we must think of a permanent home. Life in the fort is pleasant, but it's not the place to raise a family. There are no schools; there are no churches; there aren't even any missionaries."

He remained thoughtful for a few minutes as he bounced the laughing child on his knee. "You're right, Marie-Anne. Even the companies can't decide where to build their forts." He was referring to the fact that the two companies had abandoned their posts further up the river and had returned to an earlier location known as White Earth. "I can't blame them.

This is a better location to defend in case of an attack. The Blackfoot and their friends haven't been very friendly the past two years."

"What should we do, Jean-Baptiste?"

"I've been thinking. Mr. Bird tells me that one of the big bosses of the Hudson's Bay Company has purchased from the company a large area of land on the Red River, and he plans to build a colony there. Jim tells me that already a shipload of settlers have left England and should be arriving along the Red River this summer."

"But they're English. It'll be an English colony."

He paused. "That's true, but there'll be teachers...and priests...and other white women."

"Are they Catholics?"

"I don't know... there'll be children, companions for ours."

Marie-Anne looked at him surprised. What did that matter? They had many playmates now. He did not understand. It was the church—and the school that was important.

She growled, "Our children have plenty of playmates now. The children here are good. Our children are happy. But soon they'll need an education...to learn to read and write...to learn about God, and Jesus, and Mary, and Joseph...to go to church for mass every Sunday. That's what they need."

"I know that, Marie-Anne. I know that, but I don't want to go back to Lower Canada. I like this land; it's free and it's easy to make a living. I like it here."

"How long will the fort stay at this location, Jean-Baptiste? You don't know. Tomorrow the factors may decide to move again. It's hard to be forever moving. Jean-Baptiste, I want a home of my own. I've been a gypsy long enough."

He shrugged his shoulders. He looked at her and smiled. "You're right. I think we should go back to the Red River. I could hunt buffalo and sell the meat to the new people who'll be coming. Bird tells me they're farmers and they'll be cultivating the land to grow grains—wheat, barley, corn.

Until their farms are ready to support them, they'll need meat, and I'm the man who can supply them."

Marie-Anne smiled. It would be exciting to return to the Red River valley. But it would be a hard journey. She remembered the trip to the West three years before: the long hours, the cool mornings, the hot afternoons, the bugs and insects, and the wild animals, particularly the bears. Then, she had but one child; now she had three, and the oldest, Renee, was a few months over four years old. The youngest, 'Cypres', was only six months old. "Jean-Baptiste, I'm ready to leave whenever you are. I'll start to pack right away."

Jean-Baptiste laughed; it had been a long time since he'd seen his wife so eager to go on a trip. "My dear, it won't be easy. The brigades will soon be leaving for the East; maybe I can make an arrangement with Mr. Hughes at Fort Augustus. His brigade will be going to Fort Garry."

"Do you think he'd allow us to go?" Her voice rang with excitement.

The next weeks were exciting for Marie-Anne. She was busy preparing for the journey. Jean-Baptiste made arrangements to go with the brigade that would leave from the North West Company post, Fort Augustus. This brigade, unlike that of the Hudson's Bay Company's York boats, consisted of northern canoes—great birch bark canoes over thirty feet in length carrying four tons of furs and manned by a crew of ten voyageurs.

They boarded the canoes on a bright, sunshiny day in late May. The birds sang gaily, and the entire population of both forts, Fort Augustus and Fort Edmonton, were there to see them off. Although Marie-Anne was glad, she was also sad. She had made many friends during her stay in the West. She had learned much about frontier living. She had had many exciting experiences, including the birth of two children.

As the canoe carrying her and her family rounded the last bend which hid the forts from her sight, she waved vigorously to the people standing on the shore, and a tear slid slowly and silently down her cheek. She wondered if she'd ever see these people again. Then she turned her back to the forts and looked ahead down the wide, turgid river.

The next days passed quickly as the brigade followed the swift-flowing river downstream, making good time, stopping at posts along the way, and proceeding with an enlarged fleet as other canoes, also bound for the summer meeting of the North West Company at Fort William, joined them.

Each time they passed a brigade of York boats there was a great cheer from the voyageurs who jeered at their rivals with their heavy, flat-bottomed, sharp-pointed, plank-constructed boats. Most of the Hudson's Bay Company boats were manned by Orkneymen from the northern isles of Scotland while most of the voyageurs were French-Canadians, like Jean-Baptiste, or Metis, men of mixed Indian and Canadian blood. Sometimes the rivalry was so intense that it lead to fights between the crews. This seemed to be accepted as the Orkneymen were English-speaking and Protestant, while the voyageurs were French-speaking and Catholic. Most of the time the rivalry was friendly, even when the competition between the two companies was at its greatest.

By the middle of June, they arrived at Grand Rapids, where the Saskatchewan River, after flowing through Cedar Lake, rushed to its mouth in Lake Winnipeg. Marie-Anne marvelled at the roiling waters as they cascaded between the vertical walls of white limestone that were the banks of the great river. She carried the young Cypres on her back in a cradleboard, and trudged over the well defined portage trail as the other children followed behind her. Jean-Baptiste could not help her as he was one of the voyageurs whose job it was to carry the ninety-pound bundles of furs and the canoes around the unnavigable Grand Rapids.

As she tramped along the path, she was thankful that she could take her time with her children. The heavily-ladened voyageurs passed as they jogged along the trail with their heavy loads. The black flies and mosquitoes swarmed around the sweating men which seemed to urge them to greater speed. The trip on the river had been quick and uneventful, and she wondered if Lake Winnipeg would be as kind to them. She knew that if the weather remained pleasant they would be on the lake about ten days, but if it became stormy, that might become three weeks, and she didn't like that idea.

That evening, after the camp had settled for the night, she and Jean-Baptiste sat quietly before their campfire, listening to the night sounds from the lake—the lap of the water against the rocky shore, the chuckle of feeding water birds, and occasionally, the hoot of a hunting owl.

"Isn't it beautiful, Jean-Baptiste?"

He smiled to her across the dying fire. "It's the most beautiful country in the world. So large and free, unspoiled by man. The Indians have lived here for centuries and it's as if they never touched it. I wonder what'll happen to it now. Settlers from Europe are coming. They'll change it. I think they'll spoil it. They'll plough the plains; they'll fence the lands; they'll drive away the buffalo and the deer. Already the beaver are disappearing, and they're hard to trap."

"I think, Jean-Baptiste, you'll have to join them. You'll have to get some land and become a farmer. I know you're a good hunter, but I'm sure you can also be a good farmer...like your father...and my father."

Two weeks later, on a grey day with a fine drizzle, they arrived at Fort Alexander, the North West post at the mouth of the Winnipeg River. Their arrival was quiet compared to most. The weather subdued the spirit of the canoe crews, and, as well, they had not yet arrived at their final destination, which was Fort William many miles further east on Lake Superior.

The Lagimodieres had reached their destination. Jean-Baptiste had hired on to this location. He planned to stay in the West with his family. They spent the next two days resting after the long voyage. Jean-Baptiste set up their camp in the area reserved for visiting Indian tribes as there was no available housing within the fort. Marie-Anne was very busy looking after the needs of her husband and children.

The second afternoon after their arrival, Jean-Baptiste came from the post with a long face. Marie-Anne noticed it immediately. "My husband, what's the matter? You look unhappy."

"Things aren't working out the way I hoped they would."

"Why?"

"It's a long story, my love. But it seems our settlers have been delayed. The gossip is that they haven't yet arrived at the Hudson's Bay. As well, the North West Company's not happy with the situation."

"Is there likely to be trouble?"

"I don't think so, but one can never know. The Metis aren't too happy about the idea of white men coming into their country and taking land that has been used by the buffalo for hundreds of years. They fear the buffalo will disappear if farmers move in. They support the North West Company."

"Do all of them think like that?"

"No, there are many who are in favour of a colony—many of the older men of the North West Company. They see it as a place of retirement, a place where they can settle with their families and live out their last years in comfort…and in the company of their friends."

"That sounds very confusing, Jean-Baptiste. Some want the new colony; others fear it. To me, it seems to be a good thing; there'll be progress. Schools will be needed, churches will be built, mills will spring up to grind the grain and to make lumber for homes and other buildings. To me, one day this country will be like Maskinonge and Three Rivers."

"You may be right, Marie-Anne, but not all people see progress as you do. Many of these people have never been further east than Fort William. They don't want their country to change; they know nothing but trapping and hunting, and they fear that farming will ruin that, just as it has done further east."

"They can't stop change, Jean-Baptiste."

"I think they know that, but they fear it. There's much talk about this man who's responsible for what's happening."

Marie-Anne looked at him quizzically, waiting for him to continue. He reached for Laprairie who had moved toward his father. He placed the boy on his knee, carefully drawing him close. The tow-headed lad snuggled against his father's chest and stuck his thumb into his mouth.

Marie-Anne smiled at them, then asked, "Who's this man?"

"He's the chief director of the Hudson's Bay Company, a Scot lord, the Earl of Selkirk. It seems he's very concerned about the poor farmers of Scotland who've been forced from their homes because the landowners are turning the land into large sheep ranches. So they have no place to go."

Marie-Anne's brow furrowed. "He sounds like a very generous man. His concern should be praised, not condemned."

Jean-Baptiste smiled at his wife's emotion. He knew her generous heart and understood her concern for the under-privileged. "I hope all goes well. There's a rumour the settlers won't arrive until next spring. They have to winter at York Factory on the Bay. I'm afraid they'll suffer a great deal. The weather there is very cold, and there may be a shortage of food. I've been told that hunting's not good there. Well, we'll have to wait and see."

"Jean-Baptiste, what are we going to do since there are no settlers to provide with meat?"

Jean-Baptiste stroked the child's cheek and looked thoughtful. "I haven't decided yet."

During the next week, Marie-Anne heard many rumours about the settlers and the new colony that was to be established in the Red River valley. Fort Alexander was a busy place at this time of year; many people coming and going as it was the post where the brigades from the west met those from the south, from the posts on the Red River, the Assiniboine River, the Pembina River, and all the smaller rivers that flowed into Lake Winnipeg. As well, the neighbouring North West post, Fort Bas de la Riviere, had its share of visitors too, and each one had his story to tell.

To Marie-Anne it was very confusing. Many times she discussed the situation with Jean-Baptiste and tried to convince him of the need of such a colony. He was a hunter and trapper and made his living following the game, so he seemed to favour the Metis and the North West Company, while Marie-Anne's sympathies seemed to lay with the expected colonists and the Hudson's Bay Company. Sometimes they argued about the merits of each position.

One evening in late July as they sat before their campfire, Marie-Anne considered their future. She was expecting another child; it would be born during the coming winter. That would be four children, and they still did not have a home.

"Jean-Baptiste, we must decide what we're to do. We can't live the winter in this tent. I can't have a child here during the winter."

He looked up from the dying flames of the campfire. "I know that." There was an edge of annoyance in his voice. He paused and then said quietly, "I've been thinking about what to do."

"What do you plan to do?"

"There isn't much to do here, so I was thinking of moving south to Fort Pembina. It's near the buffalo lands, and even if I don't find work, we'll never be hungry because I can always provide us with buffalo meat. How would you like to go back to Pembina?"

Marie-Anne was silent. She considered his plan. In the past she had been happy at Pembina, but then her family had been small. Now it was growing, and soon she would have another addition. "If we can get a house, it'll be fine."

"Good. I'll see about getting a canoe. We'll leave as soon as possible."

They were fortunate. Jean-Baptiste was able to get a small log house within the fort, and before the snows came, he and his family were comfortably settled in the fort.

The winter passed. A new child, a son, whom Marie-Anne named Benjamin, was born. Like her other children, he was a healthy, sturdy baby.

Early one spring day, Jean-Baptiste made an announcement. "Marie-Anne, I've been hired by the Hudson's Bay Company to be their chief hunter for the year."

Marie-Anne looked up from feeding her youngest child and smiled. "That's good. At least we'll have work for a year."

"We'll have to move away from the fort."

"Where are you planning to go now? Not back to the West, I hope."

"No, but closer to the new colony. I was thinking I would establish myself on the Assiniboine River. That'll be closer to the buffalo lands and not too far from the new colony."

"Are you thinking of joining the settlers and getting some land, and building a house, and becoming a farmer."

"No, my dear, I'm not ready for that, and I don't think I can make a living doing that. I'm a hunter and a trapper."

Marie-Anne sighed. Would he ever be ready to settle down? Would she ever have a home of her own?

He continued, "But, my dear, I'll build you a little home all your own. On the banks of the Assiniboine."

"Will I have neighbours?"

"I don't know. We'll have to wait and see."

"When will this happen?"

He grinned. "I'm leaving tomorrow, and as soon as I've built our home, I'll come back for you."

"How long will that take?"

"Well…We have to go on the spring hunt, and then I'll build it. In about a month."

Marie-Anne smiled broadly. The thought of her own home pleased her. "That makes me happy," she sighed.

The next three years passed quickly for Marie-Anne. Jean-Baptiste built her a snug and comfortable log cabin nine miles upstream on the Assiniboine River from its junction with the Red River. From here, Jean-Baptiste continued as a freeman selling his produce—furs and pemmican—and his services as a hunter to whoever paid the highest price. Most of his work was for the Hudson's Bay Company or Miles McDonnell, the governor of the newly established Red River Settlement. In the summer of 1812, the first settlers arrived, ill-prepared to farm on the central plains of North America.

Marie-Anne and Jean-Baptiste felt sorry for these poor people and helped to keep them from starving that first winter. Jean-Baptiste persuaded the captains of the fall buffalo hunt to include some of the Scotsmen so they could learn how to hunt buffalo and some of the other wild animals to keep their families from starving.

But in the following years, the attitude of the Metis toward the settlers changed, and there was great resentment. Marie-Anne and Jean-Baptiste tried to remain friendly with both groups, but more and more they were drawn to the plight of the settlers. The first settlers decided to farm along the west bank of the Red River one mile north of its junction with the Assiniboine River, ten miles from the Lagimodiere cabin. The harvest was poor, and food was in short supply. Pemmican from the buffalo hunt was all that kept the settlers from starving.

The tension between the Metis and the settlers grew as more arrived each year. Jean-Baptiste kept Marie-Anne informed of events as they occurred. Many times she thanked the Lord that she and her family were far from the events that were happening.

In July 1814, a second group of Scotsmen arrived and immediately set to work preparing the land and planting crops, but the Metis harassed them at every turn—trampling their meagre fields, riding by in the middle of the night emitting fearsome screams that scared the women and children and worried the men. Rumours of possible Indian attacks and threats to burn the settlers out—probably started by officials of the North West Company who felt the settlers were agents of the Hudson's Bay Company—did nothing to lessen the fears of the colonists.

One cold December night in 1814, Jean-Baptiste and Marie-Anne sat before the cheery fire in their small cabin. The flames from the stone and clay fireplace sent wavering shadows onto the mud-chinked log walls. By the meagre light, Marie-Anne was busy sewing a pair of moccasins for Jean-Baptiste. The comfort of her small home made her think of the suffering of the poor Scot settlers.

She raised her head; her grey eyes looked toward Jean-Baptiste who sat looking into the flames, contentedly smoking his pipe. "Jean-Baptiste, how bad is the situation with the settlers?"

He continued gazing into the fire, drew on his pipe, and blew a cloud of smoke toward the fire. "It's not good. Food's scarce, so scarce the governor is about to issue a proclamation."

"What do you mean?" There was anxiety in her voice.

"Food's in such short supply that he's planning to forbid the sale of pemmican to anyone outside the colony. That's foolish."

"Why?"

"Because that'll make the Metis more angry. They'll look at that as an attempt to curtail their freedom. And, as well, the Nor'Westers will see it as a way for the English company to disrupt their food supply to their posts. It won't work. It'll cause great anger, and it won't stop the Metis from selling their pemmican to the Nor'Westers. They'll do it secretly. That's all."

"But the food's needed here or the people will starve."

"That's true, but a proclamation isn't the way to do it. Mr. McDonnell doesn't understand the situation. He doesn't understand the Metis."

"Then why will he do it?"

"He's a soldier, and he believes the only way to get something is by force. But the Metis are well organized, and they outnumber the Scotsmen. As well, they have good leaders. Young Cuthbert Grant is back from the East. He's well educated and a good speaker. The Metis'll listen to him and follow him in any direction he'll lead them. It's not good."

CHAPTER TEN

THE TROUBLES

▼

The first week in October, 1815, was Indian summer. The prairies turned yellow, and the leaves fell from the few trees that dotted the countryside. The nights were crisp, and each morning frost blanketed the landscape, yet when the sun rose the air became balmy and warm.

Marie-Anne hung the clothes to dry on the cord line strung from the corner of the log house to a frail poplar tree that stood a dozen feet away, as Jean-Baptiste rode up, his horse in a lather.

He shouted as he approached, "I've some good news for you, Marie-Anne."

She turned toward him and waited as he dismounted. "It must be very good news to make you come in such a hurry."

He took her by the arm and led her into the house. The four children ran toward him shouting a greeting. He responded, then said, "Go play. I've something important to discuss with your mother." When they had left, he said, "We're moving. We're going to Fort Douglas. You'll like it there. There are people; there's activity; you won't be lonely anymore."

She looked at him, unbelieving; for almost four years, she had been alone, with only the children and the wild animals for company, and now she was going back to a post. "Why? What's happened? Are we in danger if we stay here? What have you done now?"

"I've accepted a generous offer from Mr. Colin Robertson, the man Lord Selkirk has sent to straighten out the troubles in the colony. He's looked over the situation and he's asked me to take some important dispatches to Selkirk in Montreal."

Marie-Anne's eyes opened wide. "That's far. You'll be gone a long time!"

"Yes, I'll be gone a long time, but when I return I'll be an important man in the colony. I'll be a wealthy man. Mr. Robertson has promised me a generous sum of money as well as a large grant of land. I'll build you a large house, and I'll become a farmer. The children will go to school, and I'm sure that soon priests will come to the Red River. Churches will be built."

Marie-Anne could hardly believe her ears. After all these years, her roving husband was thinking of settling in one place. But there would still be sacrifices—she would have to wait until he had accomplished his mission. Many questions came to her mind. "When will this all happen, my husband?"

He seized her hand. "Now. Right now. We'll get ready to move right away."

She peered into his face. "Are you sure that's the right choice? Until now you've been friendly with both the Scots and the Metis. Now you've chosen. You've chosen the Scots and the Hudson's Bay Company."

He spoke slowly. "No, Marie-Anne, I've not chosen one side over the other. It's just another job. I've been hired to perform a service. If the Metis had asked me to do a similar task and had offered me the same amount for my services, I'd have taken it. I'm not for the Scots anymore than I'm for the Metis. This trouble is none of my affair."

"Jean-Baptiste, that's the way you see it. But I wonder if the Metis see it the same way. We'll be at the Hudson's Bay fort under the protection of the colony. You know as well as I do that Fort Douglas was built for the settlers. I don't like it, Jean-Baptiste."

"You'll be fine, my love. I'm only moving you to the fort because I won't be around to look after you and to provide for you. That's the reason I've made arrangements for you to stay at the fort; they'll look after you while I'm gone."

"How will you go to Montreal? By the old route?"

"I don't think so. That might be asking for trouble. If the Nor'Westers find out that I'm carrying dispatches, they might want to see what's in them. No, I'll probably take the southern route, along the southern route through the United States, then to Montreal."

"But isn't that dangerous too…the war, you know."

"Don't worry, my dear. The war's over. I'll be all right. You'll see."

Wednesday, October 11, was moving day for the Lagimodieres. For the past week Marie-Anne, with the help of Renee, who was almost nine years old, had been packing, picking and choosing carefully the things she would be taking to the fort. As she worked she mused, It's surprising how much a family gathers in a short time. Many things would have to be left behind, especially the treasures the children had gathered—home-made dolls made from pieces of wood and bundles of rushes, that belonged to Renee; bows and arrows and wooden muskets, the playthings of Laprairie; gourds and rattles and noisy drums of the two younger children. Finally, everything was packed and ready to be loaded onto the creaking, high two-wheeled cart that Jean-Baptiste had acquired to haul his loads of fresh buffalo meat and pemmican to the forts or to the settlers who bought it.

The journey took most of the day as the trail along the Assiniboine River was pocked with mud puddles from a recent rain. The children were excited and treated it like a big adventure, but Marie-Anne had misgivings. She knew that Jean-Baptiste would be gone for most of a year. The trip from the Red River to Montreal was a long one, even at the best time of the year, but he was leaving just as winter was setting in. Most of it would be on foot or horseback, through an area which was little travelled and, thus, with ill-defined trails. She was also worried about living at the fort. Fort Douglas was an English fort, all of its occupants spoke only English, unlike the other Hudson's Bay forts where there were many Canadians who spoke French or Cree which she knew.

As she sat next to Jean-Baptiste on the high seat, she muttered, "I guess I'll have to learn English now."

He looked at her peculiarly and then laughed. "It'll do you good to learn English. Soon there'll be many more people here in the valley, and I'm sure that most of them will be English."

"What makes you so sure. You told me that most of the settlers had left for English Canada and the rest had left for the Hudson's Bay."

"They did. But those who were on the way to the Bay met a new group of settlers led by Mr. Robertson and a new governor for the colony, a Mr. Robert Semple. There's new hope that the colony will survive."

"But there'll be trouble." Her voice could not hide her concern.

"I don't think so. People today are civilized. They'll solve the problems peacefully." He shrugged his shoulders, dismissing the situation from his mind. "When I get back...and I should be back with the spring brigades...I'll choose my land and sow my crops. You'll have your wish; I'll become a farmer." He slapped the reins against the horse's back, startling it, making it increase its gait for a moment, then it settled back to its accustomed slow speed.

The sun was low in the west when they approached the ten-foot palisade of the recently built fort. It had been built during the summer of 1812 to serve as headquarters and a refuge for the first contingent of Scots settlers. It had been hastily built with living quarters for the governor and several smaller log cabins for the settlers. Most of these were now empty as the colonists had built small homes on the narrow lots of land that had been assigned to them north of the fort, fronting the Red River.

The log gates were open, and they creaked through them, the ungreased axles of the cart screeching in protest. The noise was so loud there was no need to announce their arrival. A tall raw-boned, red-faced man in his mid-thirties with a long musket crooked carelessly in the elbow of his left arm leaned against the gate post and waved his right hand in greeting, calling out in a deep rolling burr, "Welcome, John-Bapteese, and welcome to all the little Bapteeses."

Marie-Anne and the children stared uncomprehending, but Jean-Baptiste waved and smiled. "A good day to you, Jock." His English had a heavy French accent.

He drove the cart into the small compound to the right along the north wall and stopped before a tiny, rough-hewn log cabin with a low roof covered with sod and yellowing grass that had finished growing for that year.

Marie-Anne gazed at the building and sighed. She would miss her little home on the prairies.

Jean-Baptiste looked at his wife, then placed his arm around her shoulder. "Soon we'll have our own home."

Throughout the winter, life at the fort seemed peaceful. Marie-Anne and her family kept to themselves. The main problem was language; Marie-Anne spoke little English and the Scots spoke no French. She lived for the day when Jean-Baptiste would return. No word was heard of him throughout the long winter, but Marie-Anne wasn't too worried. She knew that he was able to take care of himself in the wilderness. She was more concerned about the situation along the Red River. Although all seemed quiet, there was tension in the air. She knew the Scots leaders had been busy during the winter trying to gain the support of the local Indians, and they had also talked to many of the Metis to persuade them to support the Hudson's Bay Company instead of the North West Company.

In May, Marie-Anne was worried when she learned that the Metis, led by Cuthbert Grant, had captured the Hudson's Bay's pemmican boats as they came down the Qu'Appelle River to the west. She was more concerned when she heard that the Metis band had captured the Hudson's Bay post at Brandon House. The talk about the fort was hostile; the governor, Mr. Semple, was ready to attack the Metis immediately, but cooler heads pointed out that they were outnumbered.

It rained the first two weeks in June; the river was swollen, and the cart trails were wet and almost impassable, but Thursday, June 19, 1816, dawned bright and clear. Marie-Anne was busy baking bread in her small house when she heard an excited shout. A man rode into the compound and reined in his horse before the governor's quarters. He was shouting and talking excitedly. She could not make out what it was all about, but she watched nervously as a group of thirty men gathered and milled about the excited messenger.

Soon the governor, Mr. Semple, came out and waved his arms to silence the group. Then he spoke calmly, yet excitement was in his voice.

Although she couldn't understand everything that was said, what she did filled her with dread. The scout reported that a large group of Metis with carts were travelling north toward the mouth of the Red River at Lake Winnipeg. They were well armed and looked as if they intended to attack the settlement. Semple asked for volunteers to accompany him to find out what the Metis were up to. All the men volunteered, and Marie-Anne watched alarmed, as the party of about thirty-five men mounted their horses and hurried through the fort gate.

Her heart beat faster as she watched the solid gates being closed and barred. What was happening? Was this war? Her worst fears were confirmed as she watched two men load and arm the single light artillery piece that stood in the middle of the compound. They pointed it at the gate ready to repel any invaders.

During the next hours, she tried to go about her work as if nothing had happened, but she couldn't. The more she thought about the events, the more she worried. What if the fort was attacked? How would the Metis treat her and the children? Would they consider her a traitor since she was in the English fort?

She heard the shouts of several men. There was anguish in their voices. "Open up! Let us in! Quickly!. The Metis have killed the governor and most of the other men."

The gate was opened, and nine or ten men came through, shouting and crying. "They'll kill us all. We must leave. We must get our families together and leave this savage land. Or we'll all be killed. They showed no mercy. They killed everyone!"

Marie-Anne could see they were about to abandon the fort; she would be left at the mercy of the aroused Metis. Although she did not think they would harm her or the children, she could not take that chance. She must leave too. But she did not want to join the fleeing settlers. If she did, Jean-Baptiste might never find her again. What should she do?

Quickly she gathered a few necessities into bundles and gave one to Renee and another to Laprairie. The largest she shouldered herself, and then holding the hands of the two younger children, she quietly left the fort. She planned to make her way a mile south where the Nor'Westers' post of Gibraltar had stood a short time before when it had been seized and dismantled by Governor Semple in March.

The road was muddy and sticky, making walking difficult, and she could not hurry the children. She listened for pursuit, either from the Scots of the fort who might fear that she was hurrying to warn the Metis, or the Metis who might consider her their enemy because she lived in the Scots' fort. Occasionally she stepped off the rode and hid and rested in a convenient clump of willows that grew along the banks of the swollen river.

Although she was heading for the site of Fort Gibraltar, she knew it no longer existed. Governor Semple had taken over the fort in March, and he and his men had dismantled it. He insisted that all forts, in the grant of land now know as Assiniboia, belonged to the colony and only Hudson's Bay forts would be permitted. This was one of the main reasons for the Metis anger at the colonists.

She couldn't think straight. Why was she heading in this direction, southward? Pembina, the fort that she was most acquainted with, was in this direction, and it was away from the Metis as well as the Scots who planned to float down river in their boats. But what was she to do? She had little food and not much else. They were wearing all the clothes that she could put on them.

Fortunately, the children were co-operative. They followed her silently and willing as they trudged along the rutted road. Perhaps she could return to her little house on the prairies, miles up the Assiniboia River.

That idea gave her hope, and she quickened her steps in the direction where the Assinboine flowed into the Red River. When she arrived there, she'd make her decision. Head down, she plunged on.

She rounded the last bend in the road where it lead to old Fort Gibraltar. Her heart leaped. The area next to the old fort site that was reserved for Indian encampments was occupied. About two dozen tepees were set up in a ring. The camp was quiet, although the usual number of dogs roamed about. As she and the children came into view, several began to bark and move toward her. The dogs were wretched timid animals who long ago had been beaten into submission so Marie-Anne had little fear of them. Several persons who were about the camp stopped what they were doing and studied the small group walking wearily into the camp.

As she approached, she realized from the muttered comments of the watching inhabitants that it was a Cree camp. Her spirits lifted; at least she could speak their language. She headed for the largest lodge because she knew that the most important man of the camp would live in it. No attempt was made to impede her way. News of her entry into the camp spread quickly, and a circle of curious spectators watched her as she moved slowly toward the main lodge. Furtively she glanced about her. Finally she stopped before the tepee. The opening was covered with an oval moose-hide framework that acted as a door.

She called, "Oh, great chief of the Cree, may I speak with you?"

She waited. No sound came from within. She knew it would be rude to call again. So she waited.

Time passed. The curious now formed a ring around her. There were murmurs throughout the group. She caught a word here and there. They didn't sound hostile so that made her more comfortable.

Suddenly, the door covering moved on its leather-thong hinge and was pushed aside. A tall slender man in moosehide leggings and wrapped in a Hudson's Bay trade blanket stepped out.

She gasped in astonishment. It was Grey Wolf, the chief of Monique Bellegarde's band. He stood glaring at her stonily, silent, and imposing.

She bowed her head slightly and then spoke, "Chief Grey Wolf, I am the 'Great Hunter's' woman. I'm Marie-Anne Lagimodiere...and these are my children. We need your help."

"Ah, Jean-Baptiste is my friend. His woman and children are welcome in my camp. Why do you seek my help?"

"There's been trouble at the fort. Many men have been killed, and there may be more fighting. I'm not sure what happened, but the fort is no longer safe for me or my children. I'm looking for a safe place."

"The quarrel between the Hudson's Bay and the Canadians is not mine. We are at peace with both," the chief muttered. "So you are welcome in my camp. I will protect you. Jean-Baptiste did not quarrel with anyone."

Summer turned into fall, and still Jean-Baptiste had not returned to the Red River. Marie-Anne heard no word from or of him. As each day passed, she feared that he had not survived his journey. She had begged him not to go, but he had laughed at her list of dangers that he must face. He knew and understood the wilderness, and he was friendly with the Indians, the Metis, the Hudson's Bay people, and the Nor'Westers—he feared nothing.

Grey Wolf was a generous man who treated Marie-Anne and her children as part of his family. They shared his lodge and his food throughout the summer, but as autumn approached, Marie-Anne knew that she could not stay with the band. As was their custom, the band planned to head north into the trapping country along the shores of Lake Winnipeg. If she went with them, Jean-Baptiste would not know where to find her. In her heart she knew that he would return to her and the children.

Her plan to return to her small house on the Assiniboine was foiled. A roving band of Indians or Metis had burned it down. No one seemed to know for sure.

One day in early September, she told Grey Wolf, "Soon you will want to go to the trapping grounds. You've been a good friend, and I'll tell

Jean-Baptiste of your generosity, but I must stay here so he'll know where to find us."

Grey Wolf's brow wrinkled. "Here is not a safe place for a woman and four children. Where will you live? How will you feed the children?"

She smiled. "I'll manage, Grey Wolf. I know how to catch rabbits and muskrats and beaver. Food's not a problem. But I must find a shelter for the winter."

Grey Wolf's dark eyes twinkled. He admired Marie-Anne's courage and loyalty. "What if Jean-Baptiste is dead? What if he does not return? Then what will you do?"

She shrugged her shoulders. "I know he'll return." But she did not feel as sure as she sounded. Jean-Baptiste had plenty of time to return. It was a year since he had left her at Fort Douglas. "What has happened to him?" kept ringing through her mind.

Grey Wolf was silent for several moments. Then he said, "If you are sure that you wish to stay here for the winter, I know of a small abandoned log cabin one day by canoe down the river. It needs some repairs, but it will be a good home for the winter."

"Will you take me to it, Grey Wolf?"

"Yes, I will take you to it, and I will help you to get ready for winter. I will leave you a supply of pemmican, some traps, and some wire for rabbit snares, but you will have to get your own wood. That is not a chief's job."

Marie-Anne smiled inwardly. Getting wood for the fires was a woman's job; no self-respecting warrior would do that kind of work unless it was an emergency. "You're most generous, and I thank you for all you've done for me and my children."

Three days later, Marie-Anne and her family were at the small log cabin. When she first saw it, her disappointment was hard to hide. There were many chinks between the logs; the log and clay fireplace and chimney needed much repair; the sod roof had fallen away in spots; the windows needed replacing—there was a great deal of work to be done.

During the next week they worked hard to make it liveable. The last days of September was upon them, and the crispness of the fall air reminded her that winter was not far away. Each day she thought of Jean-Baptiste and hoped that he would soon return. The last week in September turned cold; a keen wind from the north brought dark grey clouds that swirled and occasionally dropped a chilly drizzle onto the dull landscape.

Late one afternoon, as she sat huddled with the children before a small fire in the clay fireplace praying the rosary, a loud knock at the door startled her. "Who is it?" she cried.

"Jean-Baptiste Lagimodiere. I'm looking for my wife and children.

In a single bound, Marie-Anne was at the door, removed the stout bar that secured it, opened it, and flung herself into the arms of her husband. He took her in his arms and held her tightly as all the tension of the past months fell from her. Her body shook as sobs shuddered from her. The children ran toward him shouting, "Papa, Papa, you're home."

He gathered them into his arms and said simply, "I love you."

CHAPTER ELEVEN

SETTLING DOWN

―――――――――▼―――――――――

The winter snows were late in coming, which suited the Lagimodieres. One evening late in October, after the children had gone to sleep, Marie-Anne and Jean-Baptiste sat before the fire in the tiny fireplace.

She looked up from the pair of socks she was knitting and smiled at him. "How long do you think it'll be until we'll be able to move into our new home?"

True to his word, Colin Robertson, before he left the Red River Settlement, made arrangements for a grant of land to Jean-Baptiste Lagimodiere. It was located on the east bank of the Red River directly across from Douglas Point, the bend in the river on which Fort Douglas was situated.

He removed his pipe from his mouth, continued staring into the flickering flames, and said, "It'll be ready next week...if the weather holds. We have to finish the thatch on the roof and a little more plastering on the outside. A few days for it to dry, then we'll be ready to move."

"We've been lucky the weather's been nice. If it'd turned cold early, we'd have had to stay here for the winter. This shack's not my idea of a home. There are too many bugs and mice living with us." She smiled. Most of the homes in the West had their share of unwanted inhabitants—mice, spiders, bedbugs, and other vermin. Marie-Anne was used to these.

Jean-Baptiste grinned. "Don't think your new house will be free of these visitors. It's just a temporary home, for now. Later I'll build the home you always wanted, my love."

She smiled and teased, "How much later?"

"Soon, maybe even next year. I've a good amount owing me by the Hudson's Bay Company. I'll make use of it to get my farm going. I've already made a deal to have a cow sent up from the United States. It should arrive next spring."

"Oh, Jean-Baptiste, that's wonderful. Then we'll have milk, and cream, and butter. Oh, that's wonderful."

The weather remained mild, and the next week they moved into their new house. Although, it was a simple log cabin, it was an improvement over the abandoned shack they had been occupying. For one thing, it had a floor of logs that had been hewn flat and which were fitted together carefully so the cracks between them were very narrow. Jean-Baptiste had even been able to get a piece of glass for a small window. The chinks between the logs of the walls were carefully filled with moss, and then they had been plastered with a mixture of clay and grass, inside or out. There was a large log and clay fireplace in the east wall of the building, and Jean-Baptiste had scrounged a tin stove from the fort. It was set up at the opposite end of the single room; Marie-Anne could use it as a cooking stove as well as to keep the room warm. Along the south wall, Jean-Baptiste had built a row of bunks for sleeping; along the north wall was a rough table and several blocks of wood used as chairs. Marie-Anne was pleased with her new home.

The first evening they spent in their new home Marie-Anne could not retain her joy. "Jean-Baptiste, the Lord has heard my prayers. Everything I've asked for is being given to me. You're safe now. At one time, I was sure you had died."

"Yes, my love, the Lord has been good to us. When I heard that Fort Douglas had been captured by the Metis and that everyone had been killed, I was sure he had abandoned me. There was nothing to live for. You were gone. The children were gone. I didn't want to come back. That's why it took me so long. I took my time."

"That was a bad time, but I never lost my faith in the Lord. The children and I prayed every day that you were safe and would return to us. He listened."

Jean-Baptiste reached across the narrow space between them and took her hand in his. "I couldn't believe it when I reached Pembina, and they told me that you were alive and that the children were also alive. I heard that Grey Wolf had given you shelter when the fort was attacked. You'll never know the joy that came to my heart."

"Oh, I know. That same joy came to me when you found us in that miserable hut. I'd never lost faith that you were still alive, but to see you again, alive and well, filled me with a great happiness. I can't remember when I was so happy."

"We're ready to start a new life," he whispered.

And start a new life, they did. During the winter, Marie-Anne was surprised by Jean-Baptiste's eagerness to become a farmer. Now that he had land of his own, he made plans to grow grain, to plant a garden, and to acquire animals, particularly, a cow, and to build a new house.

In the evenings, after the children had gone to bed, he discussed his plans with her. "I'll build you one of the biggest homes in the Red River, my love. It'll have two storeys, and two fireplaces."

Marie-Anne smiled. She hoped he would keep his promise because she always wanted a nice home for her growing family. "Do you think the troubles are over?" she asked.

"It looks that way. Everyone is very quiet now."

The winter was mild and spring came suddenly. Soon the Lagimodieres were busy on their land; Jean-Baptiste cultivated and seeded a large patch of wheat while Marie-Anne and the children worked at a large garden. To Marie-Anne's surprise, Jean-Baptiste started building a large house of square-hewn logs. She watched with interest as the structure slowly took shape—it would be a true home, and she was proud of it. It had two storeys, as he had promised, and it would require two fireplaces to heat it in winter—one at each end. The upper storey would be the sleeping quarters.

In June, 1817, Lord Selkirk arrived in the colony with ninety Swiss soldiers. They occupied Fort Douglas and impressed everyone with their discipline and fighting appearance. They had fought in the war between Canada and the United States, which had just ended. Many of them joined Lord Selkirk because he had promised them free land in the settlement.

Immediately, Lord Selkirk started making peace treaties with the local tribes of Indians, the Crees, the Assiniboines, and the Ojibwas. His presence in the colony instilled confidence and stability because he soon had it organized efficiently.

Marie-Anne watched these happenings with interest and hope. Her idea of a civilized settlement was becoming a reality. One day, as she worked alongside Jean-Baptiste in their almost completed home, she asked, "Have you heard anything from the Bishop of Montreal about the priests we asked for."

"No, I haven't, but I've heard that Lord Selkirk isn't against the priests coming into the colony."

"What do you think we should do?"

"Maybe we should write another letter to the bishop."

"Perhaps a petition would be better. I'm sure many of the newcomers would sign."

"Marie-Anne, that's a good idea."

"Could you speak to Lord Selkirk about it. You know him, and I'm sure he'll listen to you. We need priests to perform weddings, to baptize the children, and to start a school."

Lord Selkirk favoured the petition which Marie-Anne was the first to sign. Selkirk even promised to deliver it in person when he returned to Montreal.

Peace and quiet returned to the area. When Selkirk left in the fall, some of the Swiss soldiers returned with him, but most stayed and settled on the land. The colony now consisted of four groups—the Metis, the

Canadians, most of whom had Indian wives, the Scots, and the Swiss. The Lagimodieres tried to be friendly with all.

One evening late in July, Marie-Anne and Jean-Baptiste admired the produce of their garden. It had been a good year, so the vegetables had grown well.

"The garden looks good, Marie-Anne. It'll be good to have vegetables to go with the meat that I'll hunt in the fall."

Marie-Anne smiled. Although Jean-Baptiste spent most of his time this year working on his farm, she knew that he missed the freedom of the plains—the hunt, the chase for buffalo. "You mustn't miss the fall hunt, Jean-Baptiste. Buffalo is still the main source of our food. We must have a supply of pemmican for the winter. We're lucky. Our garden is good, but others have not been so fortunate. We'll need a successful hunt if we're all to survive. You're still the 'Great Hunter', my husband." Her voice rang with pride.

He looked contented. He had the best of both worlds: the freedom of the plains, the fruits of civilization.

July was almost over. Although Marie-Anne had heard that two priests were to arrive from Lower Canada, no word had been received from them. As the days passed, she became more excited. She would be celebrating her thirty-eighth birthday early in August, and she hoped she could feast that day with a Mass because her birthday was on Sunday.

"Jean-Baptiste, have you heard when the priests are to arrive?"

"It should be any day now. The last I heard was that they'd left Fort William. Have patience, my dear. They'll come."

That day they learned that the priests would arrive in two days time. Marie-Anne was overjoyed. "Jean-Baptiste, you must ride and tell everyone the priests are arriving. They must be given a grand welcome. Everyone must know so they can come to the fort."

Jean-Baptiste sighed. "Yes, my love. I know. I've already told everyone I meet about their arrival. Everyone's very excited. It'll be a great occasion. Never fear."

The arrival date came; the weather co-operated. The July sun shone brilliantly from crystal blue skies. Early that morning, Marie-Anne was up and preparing—the children were scrubbed and polished, and their best clothes were ready for she had spent days making sure that all was perfect. From material she had obtained at the post, she had made a new dress for herself and a fine shirt for Jean-Baptiste. The only thing she was sorry about was that they had no proper fashionable shoes. They wore fancy moosehide moccasins.

By mid-morning, the family made its way across the Red River by canoe to the post, Fort Douglas. Marie-Anne was surprised and pleased with what she saw. The fort was flying all its flags; the compound had been cleaned. Even the old field piece that stood near the main flagpole had been polished. A table was set up in front of it, a number of chairs and benches arranged in a semi-circle before it. Marie-Anne took Renee by the arm. "Look," she cried, "there'll be speeches!"

Laprairie grumbled, "I hope they're not too long." He was not comfortable in his best trousers and new shirt. A ten year old boy was not as interested in ceremonies as his parents. The younger children, Marie-Josephte and Benjamin, stared wide eyed at the gathering crowd of Metis in their colourful garb, the Scots in their kilts, the Canadians in a motley array of clothes, from top hats and waistcoats to fur caps and buckskin leggings, and the officials of the company in their formal suits complete with vests and cravats.

Each minute the milling crowd became larger as more people arrived. Although there was still some animosity between the various factions, it was obvious that today all differences were forgotten. The coming of the priests marked a new period in the colony's history.

The sun was high in the sky when a shout went up from those waiting at the river side. Far down river, they could see an approaching flotilla. As it drew nearer, the crowd saw that it consisted of two York boats and six accompanying canoes. Soon the number of canoes increased as many of the waiting men hurried to meet the approaching crafts. As well, dozens of horsemen followed the boats on the road along the shore.

Marie-Anne's face beamed. She whispered to Jean-Baptiste, "Oh, I'm so happy!"

He squeezed her arm gently. "I'm happy for you."

The leading York boat reached the landing, and the four oarsmen leaped into the shallow water and rushed the boat up onto the beach. Several men on the shore scurried forward to help beach the boat. Only then did the two black-robed figures seated in the centre of the boat rise.

Marie-Anne watched as the soutane-clad men moved to the front of the boat. Many hands reached up to help them disembark. As they stepped onto the grey clay beach, a joyous shout went up from the crowd.

Marie-Anne stared at the priests. It was so long since she had spoken to a priest that she wondered if she remembered what was considered proper.

The taller of the two took one step forward, removed his black wide-brimmed, round-crowned hat. The gentle breeze ruffled his dark hair. He placed his left hand on the gold crucifix which was held by the wide black sash that encircled his waist. A thick black cord running from an eyelet at the top of the crucifix encircled his neck. He took the crucifix in his hand and held it up.

"I bless you in the name of the Father, the Son, and the Holy Spirit." Many bowed their heads, and then a wild cheer rose from the crowd. After it subsided, he said, "I am Father Joseph Provencher, and this is my associate, Father Severe Dumoulin." He spoke in French, but even those who could not understand him joined in the wild cheers that greeted his introduction. Again he waited for the crowd to quiet. "We are delighted to be among you. I know that many of you have waited a long time for this moment. Now we are here to serve you. The Hudson's Bay Company has kindly given us quarters in their post so we can start our mission immediately. Father Dumoulin and I have a plan. First, we will start by baptizing all those that have not been baptized and who wish to be. Then we will regularize all the marriages that have not been blessed by the Church."

Marie-Anne's heart fluttered. At last her children would be officially baptized. They would have proper names. She even hoped that they would be the first to be baptized because her marriage was one of the few that had been performed in a church.

The next days were busy ones for the two priests. Although they had hoped to follow a plan, events did not make it possible. There were so many weddings and baptisms to perform that they had to have the people make appointments in order to keep a semblance of order.

Often they performed several weddings at one time, with couples acting as witnesses for each other. While this was going on, Marie-Anne made herself useful. She made sure the priests had everything they needed for their well-being. She made their meals and washed their clothes. While they administered to the spiritual welfare, Marie-Anne looked after the priest physical needs.

Father Provencher, although he was only thirty-one years old, was the natural leader of the two, and soon the people looked up to him with confidence and respect. He treated all fairly and considerately, and even the most difficult problems of family were handled with tact and courtesy. As he worked with the families, he soon discovered that he had a problem: There were very few baptized persons in the community so there were very few persons to act as sponsors for those to be baptized and married, as the Church required these to be baptized.

One day he said to Marie-Anne, "Madame Lagimodiere, we have a serious problem here."

For a moment she was stunned. There was fear in her eyes as she looked up into his face. "What's the problem, Father? How serious is it?"

The priest smiled at her. Her concern made him answer quickly. "Oh, it's not so serious that we can't find a solution. But it's causing some concern."

"What is it, Father? Can I help?"

"Yes, Madame, you can be a great help."

"Then tell me, Father. I'll do whatever I can."

"The problem is, dear Madame, that there's a shortage of baptized persons to act as sponsors for those who wish to be baptized. You're one of the few baptized people in the colony. Would you be so kind as to act as the godmother of these poor people?

Marie-Anne laughed heartily. "Is that your serious problem, Father? I'd be happy to be the godmother for anyone who needs one.

"You understand, Madame, that your children will have to wait to be baptized until we have suitable godparents for them. You can't be godmother to your own children."

For a moment she looked at him disbelieving. Her hope that her children would be the first baptized evaporated. Then she smiled. "If that's God's wish, then so be it. But I want my children to be baptized as soon as possible."

"My good lady, it will be done."

"May I ask a question, Father?"

"My dear Madame, it would please me to answer you if I can."

"Father, there are many children here, and they can't read or write. Do you think it would be possible to start a school for them?"

"Madame Lagimodiere, I was thinking the same thing. As soon as we have a building for the church, we'll have a school."

"When do you think that will be, Father?"

"I'm hoping it will be ready early in the new year. Many men have pledged to start a chapel. And it'll be built on your side of the river. I've even chosen a name for it. It will be called the chapel of St. Boniface."

"Oh, that's good. I'm happy about that."

"My dear woman, I am also. But for now we must get on with the job at hand. You'll be godmother to many."

And she was. Marie-Anne sponsored so many children and adults that she became known throughout the colony as "The Godmother." She enjoyed her role and was proud of it.

One evening as she and Jean-Baptiste sat on the porch of their new home, she looked across the flat lands that stretched back from the Red

River and remarked, "Jean-Baptiste, this is my land now. It's my home. Soon we'll have a church and then there'll be a school. Father Provencher told me he intends to ask the nuns to come and run it. It'll soon be like Lower Canada."

"Yes, my love, I'm afraid civilization has come to the Red River. I expect more settlers to come and drive away the last of the buffalo…the moose…the deer. Hunting will never be the same."

"But life will be better, my husband. There'll be more opportunity for our children. There's much good land for farming. One day this country will have as many people as the East. Who knows, one day it may be part of the Canadas. And we've done our share to make it so. Oh, Jean-Baptiste, the Lord has been good to us!"

Epilogue

In the years that followed, Marie-Anne and Jean-Baptiste had two more children. The fifth child was named Julie, and she was to marry a man called Louis Riel. Their firstborn, also called Louis, was to become an important leader of the Metis of the Red River when Assiniboia, the official name of the Red River Settlement, became part of the new Dominion of Canada.

Both Marie-Anne and Jean-Baptiste lived for many years on their farm on the banks of the Red River; they saw many changes before they died. Jean-Baptiste died on September 7, 1855, a few months before his seventy-seventh birthday. Marie-Anne lived for another twenty years; she died at the age of ninety-five on December 14, 1875. Both are buried in St. Boniface, which is now part of the city of Winnipeg, Manitoba.

Printed in the United States
45733LVS00008B/223

9 780595 192816